Dammit, he shouldn't have taken advantage of her like he had.

He didn't know where he'd be next week, much less the next hour. His whole life could change at this cocktail party, and where would that leave Lacey?

Would he be part of *that* family?

He couldn't say anything for a second when she entered the room. Her crushed blue gaze and the flowing buttercup sheerness of her dress with the wispy material misting over her shoulders, waist and legs took his breath away.

"What's wrong?" she asked.

"You've always been so beautiful but, right now, it's painful to look at you."

Taking a step back, her hand drifted up to her hair, where a few curls fought to stay corkscrewed. Already they were wilting, softening her features more than he thought possible, making her eyes more doelike, her lips more full and vulnerable.

"You know what to say to a girl. Don't you?"

"Not too often." Awkwardly, he made one attempt, two, to offer her his arm. Just like a gentleman would, he hoped....

Dear Reader,

Well, the new year is upon us—and if you've resolved to read some wonderful books in 2004, you've come to the right place. We'll begin with *Expecting!* by Susan Mallery, the first in our five-book MERLYN COUNTY MIDWIVES miniseries, in which residents of a small Kentucky town find love—and scandal—amidst the backdrop of a midwifery clinic. In the opening book, a woman returning to her hometown, pregnant and alone, finds herself falling for her high school crush—now all grown up and married to his career! Or so he thinks....

Annette Broadrick concludes her SECRET SISTERS trilogy with *MacGowan Meets His Match*. When a woman comes to Scotland looking for a job *and* the key to unlock the mystery surrounding her family, she finds both—with the love of a lifetime thrown in!—in the Scottish lord who hires her. In *The Black Sheep Heir*, Crystal Green wraps up her KANE'S CROSSING miniseries with the story of the town outcast who finds in the big, brooding stranger hiding out in her cabin the soul mate she'd been searching for.

Karen Rose Smith offers the story of an about-to-be single mom and the handsome hometown hero who makes her wonder if she doesn't have room for just one more male in her life, in *Their Baby Bond*. THE RICHEST GALS IN TEXAS, a new miniseries by Arlene James, in which three blue-collar friends inherit a million dollars—each!—opens with *Beautician Gets Million-Dollar Tip!* A hairstylist inherits that wad just in time to bring her salon up to code, at the insistence of the infuriatingly handsome, if annoying, local fire marshal. And in Jen Safrey's *A Perfect Pair*, a woman who enlists her best (male) friend to help her find her Mr. Right suddenly realizes he's right there in front of her face—i.e., said friend! Now all she has to do is convince *him* of this....

So bundle up, and happy reading. And come back next month for six new wonderful stories, all from Silhouette Special Edition.

Sincerely,

Gail Chasan
Senior Editor

Please address questions and book requests to:
Silhouette Reader Service
U.S.: 3010 Walden Ave., P.O. Box 1325, Buffalo, NY 14269
Canadian: P.O. Box 609, Fort Erie, Ont. L2A 5X3

The Black Sheep Heir

CRYSTAL GREEN

Silhouette®

SPECIAL EDITION®

Published by Silhouette Books

America's Publisher of Contemporary Romance

To Grandpa and Grandma Green, with my love.

SILHOUETTE BOOKS

ISBN 0-373-24587-4

THE BLACK SHEEP HEIR

This edition published by arrangement with Harlequin Books S.A.

® and TM are trademarks of Harlequin Books S.A., used under license. Trademarks indicated with ® are registered in the United States Patent and Trademark Office, the Canadian Trade Marks Office and in other countries.

Visit Silhouette at www.eHarlequin.com

Printed in U.S.A.

Books by Crystal Green

Silhouette Special Edition

Beloved Bachelor Dad #1374
*The Pregnant Bride #1440
*His Arch Enemy's Daughter #1455
*The Stranger She Married #1498
*There Goes the Bride #1522
Her Montana Millionaire #1574
*The Black Sheep Heir #1587

*Kane's Crossing

CRYSTAL GREEN

lives in San Diego, California, where she writes full-time and occasionally teaches. When she isn't penning romances, she enjoys reading, overanalyzing movies, risking her life on police ride-alongs, petting her parents' Maltese dogs and fantasizing about being a really good cook.

Whenever possible, Crystal loves to travel. Her favorite souvenirs include journals—the pages reflecting everything from taking tea in London's Leicester Square to backpacking up endless mountain roads leading to the castles of Sintra, Portugal.

She'd love to hear from her readers at: 8895 Towne Centre Drive, Suite 105-178, San Diego, CA 92122-5542.

And don't forget to visit her Web site at:
http://www.crystal-green.com!

THE KANE'S CROSSING GAZETTE

Mystery Man Hiding in Siggy Woods!
by Verna Loquacious, Town Observer

Greetings from your friendly neighborhood grapevine!

I've just received word that a stranger who suspiciously resembles Kane Spencer, our town founder, has been seen skulking about the streets. Scuttlebutt has it that our own Lacey Vedae, who has some skeletons in her own closet, is helping this mystery man by cooking him exquisite gourmet dinners and warming him with her home fires. Hmmmm. Sounds like more of a courtship than an innocent neighborly interest to this observer. What does Spacey Lacey know that we don't? Read tomorrow's column to find out....

Chapter One

Someone had been sleeping in her bed.

Lacey Vedae stepped over the threshold of *her* deserted cabin—the one located on *her* property in the thick of the snow-frosted woods—and shut the door. The sudden lack of chilled air caused her to shiver, more from a sense of foreboding than anything else.

A fire danced and snapped in the grate, sending waves of shifting light over the simple oak furnishings: two bony chairs, a square table, the rumpled bed...

What in the world was going on?

She removed her fuzzy pink earmuffs, hardly believing someone had broken into this dilapidated structure in the middle of nowhere.

None of her possessions had been filched or vandalized, not that there had been much to tamper with in the first place.

Shoot. If those darn teenagers from town had come back to use her property as a love shack again she'd—

Lacey grabbed one of those iron thing-a-ma-jigs from the fireplace, just to bolster her confidence.

The door burst open behind her, swirling a blast of whistling, flake-laced wind into the room. A voice, the tone chipped with a low, flat-plains drawl, iced her more than the weather ever could.

"Who the hell are you?" it asked.

A mix of shock and anger spiraled through Lacey, and she brandished her fireplace tool while turning to meet the intruder. "I'm the woman who's going to call the sheriff if you don't keep your distance."

The figure slammed the door shut, the altered light changing his mysterious silhouette into that of an actual human being. Half abominable snowman with drifts of light snow powdering his heavy jacket, pants and boots. Half cowboy dream with the smooth motion of a wide-brimmed hat being swept off his head in apparent respect. The gesture revealed shoulder-length blond hair and a grim, if not downright sheepish, almost-smile.

"Damn," he said, beating the felt head wear against a thigh. Melting bits of ice flew to the planked floor with every thump.

"Damn what?" Lacey asked, jabbing her weapon in his general direction to make sure he didn't come any closer. "Damn, you've been caught in my cabin?"

He stepped nearer, sending her a few stumbles backward. Dang. It wouldn't do to run away like a fluttery chicken. She'd faced her share of bullies during her life in Kane's Crossing, and she wasn't about to lose her courage now—especially since she'd worked so hard to win it back over the years.

She'd learned to overcompensate in the control department. Learned that, every time she asserted herself, the past grew more distant and less threatening.

Laccy sauntered forward, wearing her most ornery glare. The *ready-to-rumble demeanor,* as her stepbrother Rick liked to call it.

Yeah, definitely in control.

"Well?" she asked, making it clear she expected a straight answer.

Something quick and explosive shot across his gaze. Something bluer than the shade of his eyes, warmer than the sputtering fire. She almost wished she could interpret the visual pause as interest, as a "Damn, I'm not sorry I got caught in this cabin. I'm saying, 'Damn, you are a mighty hot little number.'"

Excellent, Lacey, she thought. No wonder most of the town thinks you still need to be institutionalized.

She blinked, erasing those negative thoughts. Think positive, think sunshine, think…

Control.

The stranger cleared his throat, startling her. "I didn't mean any trouble, ma'am."

Ma'am? Didn't he know she was too young for a "Ma'am"? Jeez. Twenty-seven years old and she was already eliciting matronly respect.

"Don't ma'am me," she said, narrowing her eyes and clutching her makeshift weapon.

He lifted a brow, barely sparing a glance at her war-like stance, his mouth slanting to an angle that belied his exasperation. "How about addressing you as 'missy,' then?"

"You're pretty cocky for a guy who's about to get thrown in jail for trespassing. Sheriff Reno doesn't take kindly to that sort of crime."

He shrugged, tossing his hat onto the table as if he owned the place. "Cocky never did me any harm."

Oh, what a voice. If she wasn't so suspicious of him right now, that calloused tone might've already talked her into a million things—all of them bad, too.

"Whether or not you meant trouble by commandeering my property, you need to scoot out of here." She peered around, again noting the canned goods piled on a counter near the stove, a spurt of woolen shirts peeking out of an extra-large leather duffel bag on the floor next to the bed. "Seems as if you've already gotten cozy."

As he ambled closer to the fire, he spread his hands toward the heat. His hesitation in answering gave Lacey the welcome opportunity for a second lingering once-over.

Simply put, he was gorgeous. As still and breath-stealing as a cold night settling over dusk-burnished badlands, with blue eyes, chisled cheekbones and a full mouth. Sharp-edged, rough-and-tumbled. Lacey's heart hopped away from her.

Hold on to it, girl.

"So…" she said. "You're not going to tell me how many moons you've camped out here?" She paused for him to answer.

Silence, of course.

He slipped off his jacket, revealing a homespun beige shirt that emphasized broad shoulders and a wide, muscled back, crisscrossed by a pair of sturdy suspenders. As he draped the clothing over a chair, Lacey drew in a breath, her pulse beating faster at the sight of his long legs encased by rugged tan pants that covered most of his boots.

How had a man like this ended up in her own backyard?

Lacey gathered all her common sense. In spite of her flighty reputation, she very capably ran the family feed business; she was even embarking upon a risky project that would soon raise more money for the town's Reno Center—a home for foster children. She was a woman who could preside over an efficient meeting, a woman who was strong enough to show Kane's Crossing that she was no longer the waif who'd spent time in that "clinic for disturbed girls," as her mother had called it.

She and the iron pointy fire thing definitely had the upper hand here.

"Listen, I need answers. Know what I mean? After

all, here I was, taking a nice late-afternoon walk through the woods on *my* property when I saw a light burning in the window of this supposedly empty cabin. A historic cabin, built back in the days when Kane's Crossing was first settled. No one has stayed here for years, not since those teenagers sneaked in and—''

He'd glanced over his shoulder to acknowledge her words, then, after a moment or two returned his attention to the fire. He acted as if the mute flames were far more interesting than her town lore.

''Mister?'' It was making her mad to realize she wasn't compelling him in any way. Since returning to Kane's Crossing, she always had the situation in hand—with business, with her family, with her reputation and image.

He didn't stir from the flames. ''Yeah?''

Heck, at least he wasn't comatose yet. ''Imagine my surprise when I saw that someone had taken up residence in a hovel that's about to fall down around our ears.''

''Then I suppose if I were a couple decades younger I'd be Goldilocks.''

Touché.

''This must be a real laugh riot for you,'' she said. ''How amusing to turn your back on a woman with a dangerous weapon.''

His hands dropped to his sides, and he finally turned around. The fire cast a sheen around his blond hair, tickling its length with softness and shadow. "It's an andiron, and I'm sorry."

The words were few, but obviously sincere. She could tell he was being truthful by the way he'd shrugged his shoulders slightly, enough to be brusquely awkward.

"If you're so apologetic, then leave."

He pulled his mouth into a straight line and trained his gaze on the floor. A stubborn comeback.

She sighed. "If you need a place to stay, there's the Edgewater Motel out by the highway. Its roof is much less likely to come tumbling down while you sleep. Besides, this is no palace. The only point of interest is the view." She gestured to the frost-clouded window. "Hail the Spencer estate in all its glory."

She thought she saw him flinch, but couldn't be sure. Nonetheless, he recovered quickly, his voice going back to the same deep-freeze burn she'd heard when he'd entered the cabin.

"Maybe we can make a deal, miss. Maybe I can repair this heap of an abode so it's livable again."

He was all business. It was a language Lacey preferred, one she spoke well.

"Really?" she asked, interest piqued, yet adding enough doubt to her tone to let him know that she wouldn't be a complete pushover. She'd intended to fix this place for years, but had nudged the task to the bottom of her priority pile, just like other matters.

Matters like relationships, love, loneliness.

He watched her with that cocky grin, as if he knew he'd get his way. "I only have one condition."

"*You* have a condition?" She laughed. If she hadn't still been ready to attack him at a moment's notice, she would've relished the irony of his words.

"Yeah. My condition is this: If I fix this place, you leave me alone. No questions asked."

Her heart fell to her stomach. Of course he didn't want anything to do with her. No surprise there, especially for a gal who'd probably end up an old maid anyway.

Lacey tried to appear as if his words hadn't hit that gaping chink in the armor of her self-esteem.

Connor Langley regretted the words the moment they'd flown out of his mouth. Not because he didn't need to be left alone—his reason for being in this town depended upon it at this stage—but he could see how the request killed the light in her eyes, how it paled the blush of her winter-stained cheeks.

She was damned adorable in her little snow bunny outfit, with earmuffs hanging from the fingers of one dainty, pink-gloved hand, while the other held the andiron like it was a sword gone limp. The metal thumped against her tight ski pants, which were tucked into snowboots. Her perky image was further emphasized by wide gray-blue eyes fringed by spiked lashes, a slightly tilted nose and those prim-and-plump lips.

She was cuter than any woman had a right to be, sweet as powder puffs and sugar cookies.

But Connor wasn't in the mood for the heat that stole through his body every time he looked at her. He had much heavier issues weighing him down.

Issues like the necessity of staying in this cabin, a place that offered the best vantage point of the Spencer estate.

Trying to keep any sign of urgency out of his voice, he said, "Is it a deal then?"

The woman lowered her gaze and tucked a chin-length strand of dark brown hair behind an ear. The ends flipped up, reminding him of jukebox nights and sock-hops where the girls wore poodle skirts with scarves around their necks.

"This is crazy," she said. "I don't even know your name."

"That's easy." He stuck out his palm, as if every day he encountered ticked-off women who wanted to emasculate him. "Connor Langley."

She tilted her head, seemingly testing the sound of his name in her mind. Then, she inched out her gloved hand. "Lacey Vedae."

As their fingers connected, Conn felt the electric jolt of her firm grip, even if she was wearing a protective layer of wool over her skin. Her touch was steady, no nonsense, sending shock waves up his arm, down to his lower belly, stirring into something he couldn't afford to focus on.

He let go of her before he could get burned, then took a step back toward the fire.

"What are you doing here, Mr. Langley?"

Miss—it was Miss, wasn't it?—Vedae didn't mince words. He could tell she had a core of steel the minute she'd stood up to him when he'd entered the cabin.

He shrugged, seemingly unconcerned. "I'm getting away from it all. I don't want anyone to know where I am."

"So you settled on Kane's Crossing? You must be desperate for some boredom."

Actually, he'd give his life for boredom, for the way it used to be, back in the small Montana town where he'd lived all his years. Back where he'd been engaged to Emily Webster because that's what had been expected of him. Back where his mother hadn't shriveled from cancer to almost nothing. Back where he'd been Connor Langley and nothing more.

"That sounds nice to me," he said, meaning it.

Her eyes took on a wary narrowness. "You're lying. Why should I let you stay here if you can't tell me some semblance of the truth?"

Damn. "Because I'm a hell of a handyman. That was my job back in Raintree, Montana."

She crossed her arms over her down jacket, clearly not buying his guff.

"That's the honest slant on it, Miss Vedae." He paused. "I just need to be alone."

"Hmmm." She quirked her lips, considering him. "I still don't trust you."

"Trust isn't a requirement." He almost added the dreaded "ma'am," but remembered right in time how she'd reacted to the title earlier.

Too bad his mom had bred "ma'am" into him for the length of his life. You couldn't break a thirty-three-year-old habit.

Mom. The word, the image stung because, in Montana, she was waiting for him to help her, to heal her.

Well, he wouldn't do it standing here making nice with his prospective landlord. Conn needed to take his binoculars and get back to work.

"What about it?" he asked, unthinkingly taking a step forward. He itched to run a hand along her jaw, comforting her, convincing her that he wasn't such a bad guy.

At least, that's what he'd thought up until a month ago, when he'd learned the truth about himself.

Lacey Vedae sighed and tossed up her hands. "Heck. It's not like you're living in my house."

"Right."

"And you're going to do work on this hunk of junk."

"Your obviously *beloved* hunk of junk."

She sighed. "I'll think about it."

"If you adhere to my condition, we won't even know each other exists."

She stared at him for a second, her gaze going as soft as the gray-blue clouds of a rainstorm. Something like emptiness filled her eyes for the briefest moment, then flashed away.

She walked toward the door, hesitating before opening it. "I've got plenty of supplies in my tool-shed, off the main house. Help yourself."

"Does that mean you'll keep quiet about my being here?"

Her hand rested on the doorknob, then she nodded. "For the moment."

Without another glance back, she opened the door and walked outside into the newly revealed sunshine with its glare of snow on the ground.

What had that meant? Was he staying? Going?

Questions and more questions. He was sick of asking himself, testing himself every day.

All he knew for certain was that he needed Ms. Vedae to keep his secret, to keep him hidden in this cabin in the woods.

By evening, Lacey had already thought of twenty-six ways to break Connor Langley's one condition.

She settled on the temptation of a gourmet dinner.

As her boots crunched through the light layer of snow leading to the cabin, she tried to tell herself that this was a good idea. Maybe it was the biggest mistake of her life, allowing him to stay on her property, but the businesswoman in her had pretty good instincts about people. Connor Langley didn't strike her as a terrible man—not with the way in which he'd taken off his hat to greet her, or turned his back when she'd been ready to skewer him.

Maybe he'd even be happy to see her when she

told him she'd decided he could stay on her property. It could happen.

She approached the trees, leaving footprints as she went. "He did make it clear that he didn't want company though," she said out loud. "But what kind of neighbor would I be if I didn't give him a welcome basket along with the good news?"

She hefted the loaded wicker carrier from one hand to the other. "Leaving him alone would make you a good neighbor," she answered, hardly minding that she was talking to herself. "Because he did ask you to stay away."

As she entered Siggy Woods—the dark forest that had inspired more than one town legend—she pressed her mouth into a silent line. Way back when she was fourteen, her doctor at the HazyLawn Home for Girls had warned her about talking to herself but, like most advice she'd culled from her short stay in the institution, she'd pretended to embrace the suggestion while ignoring it completely.

Her problem hadn't been too much self conversation, anyway. It'd had more to do with wanting to cry all the time, wanting to stop herself from sinking into the slow-spinning black hole of her thoughts. Sometimes, long ago, she'd ached so badly that she couldn't get out of bed come morning.

At times the darkness still lapped at the edges of her mind. But she fought it—tooth and nail. Weekly therapy sessions with her Louisville doctor as well as the steady lift of Prozac helped her, healed her.

For the most part, she was happy and settled, successful and normal—and everyone in Kane's Crossing who didn't believe her was going to be convinced whether or not it drained Lacey of all energy and resources.

Between the trunks of white-glimmer pine trees, Lacey caught sight of the cabin, its bare windows winking with an orange glow. A shadow crossed over one of the panes, causing nerves to goose her heartbeat.

Connor Langley wasn't going to be ecstatic to see her but, all the same, she couldn't help herself. Every hungry cell of her body wanted to take him in, to swarm under the thick, warm feeling of attraction, even if only for the time it took to give him this basket.

She paused at the door, blowing out a cloud of pent-up steam. Then, ready for a scolding, she knocked.

A long hesitation followed, as if he was thinking about pretending not to be home. Finally, after what seemed like eons, the door creaked open on rusted hinges.

He stood in front of her, arms akimbo, his hair tied at his nape. ''What didn't you understand about leaving me alone?''

Boy, his eyes were blue. And now that she was almost toe-to-toe with him, she could see icicle-white flecks spiking the deep color of his irises.

''I…'' She grinned, shoving the gingham-lined carrier in front of her as aggressively as she'd presented the fireplace implement this afternoon. "I wanted to tell you that you can stay in the cabin. And I cooked you dinner in apology for almost running you through with that metal thing."

"I told you, it's an andiron." Then, as he cocked a brow, Lacey wondered why she'd thought this would be such a wonderful idea in the first place.

Before he could speak, she rushed on. "I really am good in the kitchen, so you shouldn't refuse this. I've whipped up a spinach and grilled shrimp salad with a sherry vinaigrette, salmon rolls with spinach and sole with Champagne sauce and pear cake savoie. Pretty decent grub for the middle of nowhere."

She waited with what had to be a silly, hopeful please-oh-please-accept-me grin on her face.

"I'm miffed," he said.

"Well, I was puttering around the house, fixing to eat dinner myself, and I thought—"

He looked away and shook his head.

Getting the message loud and clear, Lacey set the basket on the ground, right by his boots, then turned to leave.

"Wait, Ms. Vedae."

When she peeked over her shoulder, he'd picked up the wicker carrier and opened the door a crack wider. He glanced at her, something like guilt etching the lines around his mouth. "My privacy is important to me. Understand?"

With the way he'd growled the words, Lacey wondered if he was inviting her to share the meal or trying to scare her off.

Maybe she *was* being terribly invasive. "*Bon appetit,* Mr. Langley. I'll leave you to your own company."

And back she'd go to her massive house, wondering how it had ever become so empty.

The hinges screamed as he opened the door wider. "Get in here."

Ooo, a command. If her stepbrothers, Matt and Rick, or one of her employees had talked to her in such a tone, she'd have given them a good dose of put-them-in-their-place. But with this man…

She didn't say a word. She merely tilted her head as if she'd been expecting his invitation all along and strolled into the cabin.

Into the warmth of a stranger's presence.

Chapter Two

The woman sure could cook.

As Conn bit into the last of the pear cake whatever-it-was-called, he stifled a groan of contentment. He was more used to the beef and potatoes his ex-fiancée, Emily, had whipped up for him on a regular basis. Every Sunday night after church, she'd invite him over for dinner, then they'd sit in front of the television in her parents' clapboard house, pretending that someday in the future, they might have something to talk about during the commercial breaks.

But now he was dining on food he couldn't even pronounce.

Maybe it was for the best, though he hadn't exactly been singing for joy when Lacey had shown up at his doorstep uninvited. For the second time today.

After she'd left this afternoon, he'd returned to the woods to keep his eye on the Spencer estate, cursing at the absence of activity there. Maybe the family had gone out of town. Who knew? But Conn was determined to wait, to watch and collect all the information he could before taking the next step.

Introducing himself.

And the sooner, the better. His mom was slowly dying, and he'd promised her that he'd come up with a way to make her better.

The sound of splashing wine drew him back to the moment as Lacey refreshed his glass with more Riesling. The woman had come prepared with everything.

"So, now that I've got you all liquored up, are you going to tell me why you're here?" She smiled, her eyes the same color as the sky surrounding an evening star, especially vivid against the lavender of her turtleneck.

"I thought we'd already gone over this. About ten times."

"Never hurts to ask."

"That's what you think."

She pushed the wine bottle aside, tilting her head in apparent interest, telling Conn that he'd provided a little too much information.

The lady was sharp. He needed to keep all hints of why he was camped in this cabin out of his voice.

She asked, "Is it really so awful to reveal anything about yourself? I mean, talk about hiding in your cave."

He must have seemed offended, because she added, "Mars, Venus? No? You've never been exposed to the world of Dr. Phil self-help?"

Touchy-feely garbage. Right. "I'm not into all that new age philosophy, I suppose."

The smile on her mouth froze, stiffened, then melted after a beat. "Sure. All that build-yourself-up stuff. It's not everybody's thing."

Had he said something wrong? It wasn't that he looked down on group-hug betterment; he was merely a simple man who hadn't thought much about it. "I guess I just depend more on family to tell me what's what. Having strangers feed me advice about who I am and how I can make myself different doesn't appeal to a guy like me."

Lacey folded her elbows on the table and leaned her chin on her clasped fingers, the fire casting a warm glow over her features. "You know you've provided a perfect opening for more personal queries. If I didn't know that you'd scowl at me, I'd ask you what kind of guy you are."

"Are you posing an off-limits question? Because I feel that scowl coming on."

She grinned, making Conn wish she hadn't already become such a vital part of his plan to be here in the woods. If she were an anonymous woman in a roadside bar, he might be able to caress the heart-shaped angles of her face without considering the consequences. But, even now, at a point when they still barely knew each other, he couldn't afford to get close, to alienate her with the eventuality of his leaving town once he'd gotten what he needed from the Spencers.

"I can guess at what sort of guy you are," Lacey said. "You're a hiker, a nature boy who wanted to get out of the cold and ducked into my cabin. Right?"

He didn't correct her, thinking she'd concocted a pretty good cover for the real reason he was here. "And what about you? Are you the type of woman who cooks dinner for a family in that big house of yours?"

Not that he thought she would've been dining with him if she had kids and a significant other; he was just surprised he cared enough to ask.

Lacey seemed taken aback by his inquiry. "I've got plenty of kin and friends. And there's almost always someone in my home with me."

"I take the hint, Ms. Vedae. You're protected from creatures who wander in the woods and take up residence in your cabin. Don't worry. I'm not a burglar or a bad man."

She sat back in her chair, arms crossed over her chest, suddenly serious. "If I thought so, you wouldn't be here eating my fancy food. And people who can sit through one of my meals generally call me Lacey. Okay?"

"Got it." He felt as if he'd climbed over the tip of a mountain, surpassing an obstacle, enjoying the view on the other side. Even if only a small barrier had been crossed with this woman, it was a victory. Hopefully he'd put an end to her curiosity of the unknown. Hopefully she'd stay away.

He patted his stomach, as if signaling an end to the supper, but his companion merely sat in her chair, assessing him.

"There's not much to me," he said. "Just a nature lover. Remember?"

"It's not that. It's… Well, my stepbrothers will go nuts when they find out I'm letting you stay here. They're going to want to investigate."

"So don't tell them."

Lacey lifted a finger in the air, her eyes lighting up with a new realization. "You're more than a hiker. You're a hider."

"I don't like to be bothered, is all."

The words froze in the air, stiffening her posture in the process.

Lacey started to rise from her chair. "I'll just leave you alone then."

He could imagine her trooping through the snow, back to her mammoth house. Intuitively, he knew no one waited for her back there. Otherwise, why would she be eating dinner with *him?* The thought of her staring out a window at the empty, blank spaces of silent-night snow made his chest thud with his own sense of isolation.

"Stay," he said softly.

Her eyes widened, and she settled back into the seat with a certain amount of rebellion in her tight movements. Conn chided himself for listening to the angel on his shoulder. Now he'd be stuck dodging more questions from his inquisitive visitor.

After a pause, she said, "Things have gotten a tad boring since Daisy and Coral Cox moved out a few months ago. Of course, now Coral has her own little place and Daisy married my brother Rick, so..."

She caught herself, laughing. "My family. I can't stop concerning myself with their lives."

She'd said it with such patent longing that Conn couldn't help filling the silence with conversation, just to keep her talking and smiling. He'd always been such a sucker for a pretty girl.

"What do you do with yourself, besides cooking like a dervish, I mean?"

She brightened. "I run my family's horse feed business up in Louisville. But, as my brother Matt is fond of saying, I'm a master of delegation. My other brother Rick flies me in his Cessna to the city a couple times a week to take care of business, but things run so smoothly I can do most of the work from my home office."

"A corporate type. I should've known from the way you handled matters this afternoon that you're used to being in charge."

"Was I terribly overbearing?"

Conn shrugged, underplaying his first impression of her. A soft bunny with fangs.

"Not overbearing, I guess. Surely in control."

She tilted her head proudly, as if thrilled to project such an image. "Thank you."

"Much obliged."

Lacey sat up straighter, and Conn couldn't help feeling good about making her wariness disappear. He didn't know what exactly he'd said to work that magic, but the glow in her eyes was worth it.

Even though he wasn't supposed to give a tinker's damn.

The fire flickered and frost shrouded the window, emphasizing the cabin's cozy intimacy.

"Can I tell you something crazy?" she asked.

"I suppose." Was the romantic atmosphere getting to Lacey, too? Was it convincing her that they knew each other better than they actually did?

She leaned toward him again, her skin flushed. "This is so…" A hesitation, a stretched second of thought in which she bit her lip, then grinned. "I'm building a glass castle," she said proudly.

Conn tried his best not to seem jarred by her statement. He was sure he'd done a decent job of keeping a straight face, but he couldn't restrain his curiosity. "A full-scale castle? With *glass?*"

"It won't be Locksley Castle, really."

"Locksley Castle?"

She gestured with her hands, conveying her enthusiasm. "You have to see it someday. On the outskirts of the town, we've got an actual castle. An incredibly rich East Coast family with ties to European royalty lives there, supposedly, but we never see them. It's one of those Kane's Crossing myths."

Conn nodded, still not understanding the reasons

behind the glass castle, not really even understanding why she was confiding in *him,* a near stranger.

Lacey continued, unfazed. "My castle will be large enough to fit in a warehouse. I know—it sounds wild. And when my brothers first found out that I'd purchased land with the old toy warehouse on it, they thought it might be a sound investment. But then they realized I was going to hire an architect and contractors to actually build a glass castle, and they about flipped."

"What's the purpose?"

"Purpose?" Lacey's gaze drifted to the fire, as if the flames held pictures of the finished product, the crystalline structure glimmering with every cinder-sparked burst. "I wanted to do something for Kane's Crossing. Something that might bring the town together. And the Reno Center, a place for orphans, always needs money to help run it. I thought I could build this—I don't know—spectacle, and people might come all the way to our town and pay to see it."

Now the idea made a little more sense. "But…?"

"Yeah, I know," she said, waving a hand toward him to brush off his doubts. "Why a glass castle? Everyone asks me before shaking their heads and rolling their eyes. But that's why I think folks will come to see it. Because it's so…unexpected."

And majestic. Conn wasn't much into fairy tales and happy endings, but he could imagine a person staring at Lacey's creation with as much fascination as he stared at the North Star. He could even see someone making a wish on Lacey's dream.

Oddly touched and intrigued, Conn bent forward, reaching out to run an index finger over the soft curve of Lacey's cheek.

She already had a way of doing this to him—making him not think. It was scary how dumb he got when she was around.

Her eyes went wide as his finger traveled down her skin to the line of her jaw, to the tip of her chin. Conn, himself, even felt a little startled, his pulse kicking and screaming through his veins.

Suddenly, he pulled back, standing with such force his chair scraped the floor with a yelp. "Let's get you home."

One of Lacey's shoulders—the one below the cheek he'd caressed—drifted upward, as if she wanted to wipe away his touch with a brush of her turtleneck but didn't have the bad manners to do so. Was she angry because he'd been so forward?

After what seemed like an uncomfortable infinity, Lacey stood to clean the table, and he wasn't any closer to an answer.

"I'll take care of that," he said, needing to get her out of here and back to the boundary of her own house.

With a glance that seemed to chastise him for ordering her around, she left the table and retrieved her coat. She moved toward the door, and he followed.

"Forget it," she said, opening the door and letting in the night. "I can walk myself home."

She left so quickly he couldn't even thank her for dinner.

The next day, after Conn had beat himself up all night about offending Lacey, he still hadn't forgiven himself.

As he perched by a pine, he held the binoculars to his sight, training the lenses toward the Spencer estate. He needed to be disciplined in his efforts, needed to clear his mind of the cute-as-snowflakes Lacey Vedae. The stakes of his stay in the woods were too high to fool with.

He couldn't let his mother down, and the point had been driven home yet again after talking to her on the phone this morning. He'd traveled over county lines to the next town, just to stay away from the Kane's Crossing scene, using a random pay phone to check in on her. During their short conversation, she hadn't been able to hide a cough, had merrily scolded him for worrying about this minor cold.

But every sniff, every sigh worried Connor. A relapse. Death. He wouldn't let either one of them happen to his mom.

He glanced at a mild sky still cloudy enough to preserve some snow then shrugged into his coat a little more, coveting its warmth.

This damned spying was tedious, barely better than his research trips to libraries in the neighboring counties, trips that allowed him access to old newspaper files. He was determined to find out all he could about the Spencers.

The name caused the bile to rise in his throat. All these years, living a lie. All this time, thinking that he was…

Wait. A black Lexus had pulled onto the circular driveway in front of the Spencers' colonial mansion. The structure resided on a hill, as regal as a ruler on a throne, its front facade guarded by pine trees. Siggy Woods, where Conn now sat, offered a side view of the estate, allowing him to see the front and back of the house. Luckily, the trees were sparse from this point, giving Conn his first glimpse of the man he thought might be Johann Spencer, the family's new leader.

From gossip columns, Connor knew that Johann was a distant European cousin of Horatio, Edwina, Chad and Ashlyn. He'd purchased all their remaining properties after Horatio had run into legal troubles and fled to Europe.

Through the binoculars, the new token of power seemed like a giant, towering over his wife and two children. His pale blond hair clashed with the black of his expensive overcoat, offering Conn the chance to scoff at the juxtaposition of lightness and darkness contained in the same space.

But as far as Conn was concerned, the Spencers were all about darkness.

A chauffeur drove the car away as Johann led his

family toward the mansion. The front door seemed to open on its own, but Conn knew it was probably a butler who had done the menial work, ushering the Spencers into the house.

A slight shudder scampered up and down his spine, an unpleasant reminder of time running out. It was all well and good to sit here spying on Johann, but Conn needed to take the next step.

To figure out what he was going to do now that Johann was home.

As he stood, he let the binoculars drop to his chest, the item hanging there by its strap. He wasn't the kind of guy who played intrigue games. Hell, only a few weeks ago, he'd been Raintree, Montana's resident fix-it man, the one you called when you needed a roof patched or fence mended.

Conn was out of his element here.

He started to walk back to the cabin, not knowing what to do next. That's when he heard it. The sound of laughter, of children, floating through the woods with pixielike gaiety.

Kids. He and Emily had planned on them. After all, that's what you did in Raintree. You got married, had children, then called it a life. But after Conn had found out the truth about himself, had come to doubt who he even was, Emily had decided that he'd changed in some indefinable way. She'd called him a stranger and broken off the engagement.

Oddly enough, it hadn't hurt very much. By the time she'd given back the modest gold band she'd chosen from a jeweler to symbolize their union, Conn had already been numb. He hadn't had time for more bad news.

He'd actually wondered whether or not he could ever feel again.

As Conn kept walking, he realized that he was gravitating toward the young laughter.

He saw the house first, in the near distance. Lacey's place. A two-leveled stone-and-log home with green trim highlighting the arched roofs. A porch circled what had to be five-thousand square feet of space, and Conn could feel the workman in him catch fire.

He'd dreamed of homes like this, but had never come close to living in one. The fact that a lone woman wandered all those rooms by herself almost cut his heart to shreds.

As he came nearer, he saw two kids—a boy and a girl—running around Lacey, who was covering her eyes with gloved hands. The children squealed with delight and, when Lacey uncovered her gaze, their laughter intensified, squeezing Conn's throat with an unidentifiable longing.

She chased them in circles until they all ended up in a heap on the flake-blanketed ground. Then, as if in silent agreement, the three of them started waving their arms and legs, creating snow angels.

The boy finished first, hopping to his feet to inspect his creation. But that's not all he peered at.

He pointed at Conn and began to run toward him.

"Taggert!" yelled Lacey.

But it was too late. The kid had already discovered him.

"Taggert, you get back here!" Lacey yelled.

But it was fruitless. The adopted son of her childhood friend, Ashlyn Spencer Reno, and Ashlyn's husband, Sheriff Sam Reno, sprinted toward the woods with a firm mission in mind, no doubt. Tag was always letting his energy get him into more trouble than naught.

She heard the nine-year-old wailing, "The Man in the Woods!" as he faded into the trees.

Her heart froze as she squinted her eyes, barely catching sight of—indeed—a man standing on the fringe of the pines, watching them.

The Siggy Woods Monster, also known as the Man in the Woods, was one of those Kane's Crossing myths, like the Locksley Castle, that colored their town with flavor. She'd lived on the edge of these pines for a couple of years now and had never seen, nor been afraid, of any legend.

But, just the same…

"Taggert Reno!" she yelled again, walking toward the woods. "Your mom's going to hear about this!"

"It's no use," said seven-year-old Tamela Shane.

Lacey stopped and peeked down at her niece, the daughter of her stepbrother Matt and his wife, Rachel. The little curly-headed moppet had withstood a lot this past year—the return of her amnesia-afflicted father, his memory recovery and the reunion of their

CRYSTAL GREEN   37

family—but Tamela was a trouper. Lacey took inspiration from the girl every day, admiring the child's strength.

Strength. Lacey needed every ounce of it when it came to dealing with the citizens of Kane's Crossing. They'd been poking fun at her glass castle scheme since day one, ribbing her about going back to the clinic because she was still "crazy," still had "mental afflictions."

Tamela grabbed her hand. "Tag's stubborn, Aunt Lacey. He won't come back unless the Monster eats him up and spits him right back out at us."

A thought slapped her. Man in the woods. Connor was in the woods.

Elation filled her up for a moment, then deflated. He'd touched her last night, trailing a finger down her skin as if appreciating the fine grain of a wooden beam. He'd pulled away just as unfeelingly, too, as if deciding that the material wasn't suitable.

But why did his opinion matter to her? Men like Connor, ones who seemed so strong and together, didn't want women with her flawed baggage anyway. Better to have him pull away from her now rather than having him reject her when he found out she'd enjoyed a restful mental vacation at HazyLawn.

By this time, Tag had managed to drag the man out of the woods and, as expected, it was Connor.

If the guy didn't want to be bothered, what was he doing here?

"Aunt Lacey," said Tamela. "The Man doesn't seem so scary."

Exactly, and that was the frightening thing. With his bulky coat broadening his shoulders, his wide-brimmed hat hiding all but that blond ponytail, his slow-molasses gait as he allowed Taggert to drag him out of the woods, Connor Langley was the scariest creature Lacey had encountered in a long time.

Maybe even more horrifying than the dark-robed ghosts who knocked at the entry to her dreams most nights. Ghosts she'd left behind as a teenager: severe depression, unworthiness, emptiness.

As Connor came nearer, a distant part of Lacey wanted to return to a protective shell, the shell she'd destroyed after returning to Kane's Crossing, to a family who embraced her and everything she'd gone through.

Yet instead of cowering, Lacey gathered her strength while Tag introduced her to the man hiding in her cabin.

Chapter Three

An hour later, Lacey watched through the kitchen's glass window while Connor helped Tag and Tamela put the finishing touches on something they called a "snow wookie." It resembled a cross between a fuzzy dog and a long-limbed giant but, hey, the kids loved it.

Connor laughed—actually laughed—as he held up Tamela so she could meticulously sculpt the wookie's plush lips. Lacey couldn't believe this was the same man who grimaced at her every time she asked him a personal question.

But she ended up smiling, too, his happiness tickling her.

They finished their work of art, standing back, the

children checking to see if Lacey was paying attention by waving at her. She gave a thumbs-up sign and continued with her hot cocoa preparation.

Moments later, they'd disappeared, and Lacey could hear them in the mudroom, stomping the snow off their boots. Then, they entered the kitchen, Tamela and Tag trailing Connor, their eyes fixed on him with a fascination you could only get away with as a child.

"Your creation is really something," Lacey said, handing the steaming beverages to the kids. Tag grabbed his mug with one hand, since the other was merely a nub—a disfigurement he'd been born with, not that it mattered in the least to him.

When Lacey gave Connor his cocoa, she tried to avoid his gaze, but failed. Instead, they locked glances, both of their hands on the mug.

Adrenaline surged around her heart, poking at it, reminding her that it had been a long time since she'd been this attracted to a man. In fact, Lacey couldn't ever remember a feeling this intense, not even with the one serious postclinic boyfriend she'd dated, made love with, been rejected by.

"Much obliged," he said, still looking at her while bringing the drink to his lips.

Tamela started walking into the living room, where Lacey had stoked a roaring fire. "Tell your friend to help us with the origami."

"I'm sure my friend would like to relax." Lacey followed the kids into the next room. A floor-to-ceiling window lent light to the area, emphasizing hickory floors and lodgepole-pine-logged walls. The stone fireplace, with its built-in mosaic of faded oriental-themed tiles, dominated the room. She wondered if Conn would think her taste off-kilter. She wondered why she cared.

Tamela sighed and settled on a thick rug across the large room with Tag to practice the Japanese art of folding paper into shapes. Lacey had taught the kids origami for baby-sitting days like this, when her family and friends needed "couple time" with each other.

As the children began their task, the Renos' two cuddly Maltese dogs wandered over and nestled against Tag and Tamela, completing the cozy picture.

Lacey sat on an overstuffed couch opposite the fire, and was surprised when Conn took a place next to her. For a full five minutes they merely watched the kids manipulating the squares of paper, Tamela helping Tag when he needed it.

Conn turned to her. "I didn't mean anything by last night. Didn't mean any hard feelings."

"Of course not." Did they really need to hash this out?

"Good," he said, evidently thinking they were clear on the matter. "I don't want ill will between us."

She shook her head. "You make no sense to me."

"That's a good way to keep it."

She kept her voice low, so as not to include the kids in the conversation. "Why in tarnation are you in my house, Connor? I thought you wanted to hide in that cabin.''

He paused, then laughed. ''I got caught. By a little kid, no less.''

''So much for being a hermit.'' It occurred to Lacey that he might crave companionship as much as she did. Who wouldn't in the cold of winter, when everything seemed so bleak and removed?

She continued. ''I thought you didn't want anyone to know where you were. Instead, you advertise your presence.''

Conn rested his mug on a thigh, drawing Lacey's gaze to the firm muscles beneath his tan pants. She glanced away.

He said, ''I told Tag and Tamela I'm an old friend who was driving through town and wanted to say hi to you. That should cover any questions your relatives might ask.''

''Yeah. You've got everything covered.''

''Lacey.''

Reluctantly, she looked over at him, regretting that every peek made her heartbeat thump a little faster, made it harder to catch her breath.

His hand drifted up, then jerked back, almost as if he wanted to touch her face again. Lacey's belly warmed as she recalled last night's fleeting caress.

''Don't be angry with me,'' he said. ''I don't want to talk about why I'm here or why I want to be left alone. All you need to know is that I'm not going to do anything to cause you harm.''

Didn't he know his presence made her question her loneliness for the first time in years? And that, in itself, caused her plenty of pain?

A resounding knock on the kitchen door forced Lacey to bolt out of her seat. "I've got it."

She left Conn sitting by himself, staring into the fireplace. Appropriate, since he wanted to be alone anyway. Didn't he?

On the way to the other room, she passed the kids, who were still immersed in their art.

As she entered the kitchen, she saw a shape filling the door's window. A husky, rag-padded woman with a ruddy complexion and slanted black eyes. The lady, known around these parts as The Wanderer, smiled, showing a gap where her two front teeth used to be. She resembled one of those apple dolls, skin sucked in and shriveled, clothed in tattered threads and third-hand shoes.

Lacey opened the door, knowing the old woman wouldn't enter her kitchen. "How are you tonight, ma'am?"

"Fine as can be, Miss Lacey."

She went to a cupboard, where she always kept a prepared sack of food for The Wanderer. The old woman didn't come around more than a couple times a week, and Lacey felt compelled to help however she could, especially since most people in Kane's Crossing liked to make-believe the homeless woman didn't exist.

The elderly lady took the sack, bowing her head. "You're a kind one."

"Nonsense. I only wish you'd let me do more." Usually, at this point, she asked The Wanderer if she had somewhere to sleep, if she'd like to stay in the cabin in the woods, but Lacey bit her tongue.

The old woman cast her a glance that clearly told Lacey she'd noticed the omission in their ritual, the lack of cabin talk. Then, after a beat, she said, "Well, thanks much. I got places to go."

"You have a safe week."

Lacey watched The Wanderer hobble away, wondering where the woman spent nights, wondering who she used to be—who she was.

God, Lacey had so much to be thankful for. A home, a family, her health…

She returned to the living room, bending down to give the kids a hug on the way inside.

Tag, like most boys his age, squirmed away, continuing with his project, oblivious to her emotional flare up. Lacey stood again, unable to hold back her grin, then headed back toward Connor.

His seat was empty.

Tamela piped up. "Your friend's not here. He mussed up our hair like my dad does, then up and left."

Lacey picked up his empty mug and looked out the window at the white landscape. Why had she expected him to stay? He was a stranger, a guy who'd holed up in a cabin on her property and that was that.

He'd made it clear he didn't need company. Heck, even now, he was probably huddled in front of his own fire, alone, staring into the flames without anyone to talk to.

But she shouldn't worry about Connor. No, indeed. Because, in his exclusive club, it was obvious that no emotional ties were required there.

Day turned into night, then back into an inevitable tomorrow.

Connor found himself at the edge of the woods again, staring through his binoculars at the Spencer estate.

He was so absorbed in his boredom that he failed to hear the footsteps.

"Wow," said Lacey's voice. "This is progress. I see you're working up a sweat to repair my cabin."

Conn whipped the binoculars away from his face. Too late; she'd obviously seen them. "Taking another nature walk?"

"As a matter of fact, yeah, I am. I get cooped up in the house, preoccupied with the business. I think you felt stifled, too, yesterday, when you disappeared without even a goodbye."

He chuffed, more because of disappointment in how he'd handled himself. Sure, he'd gotten muffled by the hearth-warmed intimacy, had felt the need to get out before he was trapped by firelight and Lacey's presence. He'd also wanted to avoid whoever had been knocking at the kitchen door.

Lacey held her hands out to her sides, whirling around with a light laugh. "Besides," she added when she'd finished, "the sun's out, and it's a beautiful day for spying. Isn't it?"

He wanted to deny it, but that would be ridiculous.

She pointed to the binoculars. "What's going on?"

Damn. If he told her about his preoccupation with the Spencers, he'd lose the advantage over them. She had the potential to reveal his presence, to show his hand before he was ready to take further action.

If he'd ever be ready.

He brushed off the thought. "I'm bird-watching," he said, trying to sound convincing.

Lacey ran her gaze over the silent trees, making a show of hunting for the supposed birds. He should've been riled with her and her nosiness, should've been ready to order her to leave him alone, once and for all.

But Conn didn't have the heart. He didn't mind taking a minute to just drink her in, with her lively red scarf wrapped around her throat, with a matching headband holding back her flipped-up brown hair and covering her ears from the cold. Her skin was so wind-kissed that he wanted to cup her face in his hands, warming the chill away.

"Bird-watching," she repeated. "Exciting stuff. I, personally, would rather keep an eye on those Spencers."

Conn's spine went ramrod straight.

She continued. "Ages ago, when we didn't know

any better, Ashlyn Spencer and I used to play in these woods together. Heck, she always wanted to distance herself from her family anyway, so we never minded how her father used to yell at her for lowering herself, keeping company with the townspeople. I, myself, never had any problems with the Spencers. Not until Johann took over the family's holdings recently."

Conn was hungry for more information. His blood boiled beneath the surface of his skin, yet he tried to act like he couldn't care less. "Sounds interesting. But I'm out here to enjoy mother nature."

"Undoubtedly." Lacey came to stand next to him, turning toward the Spencer estate herself. "Remember that glass castle I told you about?"

"How could I forget?"

She smiled. "I know—it's wild. And more of a problem than I ever thought it would be. The Spencers used to own the land I bought for the castle, and now they're trying to strong-arm me into selling it back to them."

Conn's interest was definitely piqued. "Great ventures take great risks. Don't they?"

Lacey peered up at him in apparent wonder. "Exactly. I tell myself the same thing every morning. Then I tell myself the Spencers aren't going to get that land back." Strength supported her words. "Not if I can manage it."

Ironic. Conn had been doing research in libraries, spying on the Spencers, when all along he should've been pumping information out of this woman.

He needed her more than he could've predicted. "I thought maybe I could come by your place, get some of those tools tonight, start work on the cabin in the morning."

Lacey nodded. "I might conjure up a pretty good dinner if you happen to be around at seven o'clock."

"If I happen to be around," said Conn, "I'll be sure to knock on the kitchen door."

"Then maybe I'll see you tonight."

"Maybe."

She walked toward her home, and Conn watched the sway of her slender hips under her tight ski pants.

He wondered if she would rescind the invitation if she knew who she'd just asked to dinner.

Okay. Maybe she'd gone a little too far with the lit candles and Spanish guitar music.

As Connor sat at the other end of the pine table in her ambient-glow dining room, he appeared as comfortable as a nail at a hammer convention. He caught her staring, then nodded in response.

"The food's great."

She smiled at the compliment; her culinary efforts made her proud. But instead of talking around the subject once again, maybe some straightforward conversation wouldn't do any harm. "When I cook, I go all out."

Overcompensation—the story of her post-Hazy-Lawn life.

She added, "The candles and music only add to the menu."

Sure. Was it the Chicken and Sausage Paella with the *Patatine E Carote* in *Salsa Verde* that had inspired her? Or had she been thinking more about Connor's blue eyes and let-me-undo-that-ponytail hair?

Potatoes and carrots indeed. It was the eyes and hair that had caused the overkill.

This afternoon, when she'd caught him spying on the Spencers—or, er, *bird-watching*—Connor had taken one step up on her mystery-man scale of attraction. She couldn't help it. The man hid secrets, and Lacey had always been a pushover for guys who reflected her own position in life.

Her doctors would've told her that she was sabotaging relationships before they started, that her self-confidence chose men who were impossible to win over in the first place so it wouldn't be her fault when they rejected her. She was protecting herself from hurt. Well, duh.

But old habits were hard to break.

The only thing she could think to do was enjoy Connor's company while she could, then forget about it. After all, if they ever got to the point where they talked about her past, he'd be out of her life lickety-split anyway.

Connor had already finished his meal and was casting an appreciative gaze around the room. "I envy you. This is the kind of place I've always dreamed of. Hell, I'd be happy if I could just *build* a house like this.''

"That's right," she said. "The handyman from Raintree. Of course you'd be fascinated by it."

"Aren't you?"

"Oh, sure. But I didn't have much to do with the construction." She tried to see the room from his point of view, tried to take a fresh gander at the arched hammerbeams, skip-peeled posts and beams, milled logs. "I was lucky enough to buy this place after taking over my family's company. But I've added some touches here and there."

Connor fixed her with one of his spiked-through-the-heart gazes. Lacey felt the heat rise from her belly to her face.

"You mentioned your brothers. How is it that you run the business and they don't?" he asked.

"Phew. That's a long story."

"I've got time on my hands."

"All right," she said. "You asked for it."

She used her fork to push around some rice from the Paella on her plate, and decided to start her story after her stay in the clinic. She didn't think he'd want to know about it anyway.

"Here's the abridged version. My mom, who'd been wed twice before, married into the Shane family, and we moved to Kane's Crossing. I wanted—*needed*—something to excel at, and the business was it. My stepdad delighted in my interest and mentored me to succeed. He died of a heart attack running

Shane Industries and, at first, it seemed like my step-brother Matt would take over from there on out.

"Matt did a good job for a while, but started following in Dad's footsteps. He worked so hard that he alienated his family. Then one day, he disappeared and no one knew what happened to him. That's when I took over."

"Damn," said Connor. He'd leaned his elbows on the table, listening to her. The candlelight flirted over his sun-tinted skin, making Lacey long to touch the planes of his cheekbones, the shadow of a beginning beard.

She cleared her throat. "Yeah, well, Matt came back last year, but that's another story. Suffice to say that he, his wife Rachel, Tamela and the baby in Rachel's tummy are one big happy family again. Especially since Matt decided I should still run the company."

"You have another brother, though. Right? What about him?"

Lacey smiled at the mention of Rick. She'd always held a soft spot for her smart aleck brother. Not that she didn't love Matt, too, but they'd never been as close.

"Rick's another long tale. He and Dad had a falling out years ago, and Rick joined the army and fought in the Gulf War. He never wanted anything to do with the business, so he asked me to run it. Good decision, too, because now he has his own happy ending with Daisy, the woman he just married."

"And that leaves you," Connor said softly.

She wished he hadn't caught on to that part. Had she told her stories with such obvious yearning for someone to treasure *her?* Was it so clear that she didn't belong to anyone?

"I'm fine on my own," she said. "I've got lots of work to keep me busy. And I can make it by myself, especially since Dad left me a tidy sum of money when he passed away."

"Oh." Connor broke eye contact and stared at a candle, as if suddenly realizing she was a bread winner and he was a...what?

What the heck was he?

He must've sensed the question balancing on the tip of her tongue, because he said, "As for me, no epic stories. I'm just a simple guy."

If the muscles in his jaw hadn't jumped after the comment—an action similar to the kick of a rifle after it fires—Lacey would've let the words fade.

"You're not fooling me, Connor."

He leaned back, silent, watching her as intently as he'd been watching the Spencer estate this afternoon. Lacey wanted to glance away, to disengage before the look stretched into discomfort. She didn't want him peering too hard at her, because there was so much to hide.

She broke the tension. "What?"

"Nothing. Just looking."

"You do a lot of that."

"You're a very pretty woman."

Lacey tried not to act surprised. It was the last thing she'd been expecting him to say. Embarrassment crept up her neck.

"Thank you," she managed to say.

Connor shrugged, as if it meant next to nothing.

Lacey was more than aware of the fact that she talked too much when she felt under the spotlight. Probably because she'd slung so much bull at her doctors when they expected answers that she hadn't ever learned to break the habit.

"Usually," she said, her voice an octave higher than usual, "I have to deal with this whole 'cute' label. You know, like a cheerleader or kitty cat or bunny—"

Connor's brows lifted.

"—but it's a relief to hear someone say 'pretty' instead of 'cute.' Not that I look in the mirror every morning and ask, 'Who's the fairest of them all?' Because I don't care much about that…"

She let the sentence trail off into the air. What a ditz.

But then Connor came to her rescue, changing the subject. "You're dressed differently tonight."

Lacey looked down at her attire. For the last week, she'd been on a sixties ski-princess kick. Tonight she was riding the wave of her menu and cultivating a Spanish style, with her hair pulled back into a small, sleek bun and her silken, flared red dress covered by a black, fringed shawl.

Her propensity to change images tickled the people

of Kane's Crossing, but Lacey liked the fact that she had control over the way she appeared to them. The more she manipulated her appearance, the less power they had to shape it.

"I get a bit bored with the same wardrobe," she said, leaving it at that.

"Hell. Candlelight, music, gourmet food..." Connor stood from his chair, grabbing his plate as he prepared to clear the table. "If I was the type who loved 'em and left 'em, I think I'd be completely overcome with your charms."

Wings seemed to flutter in her belly, then stopped, a heavy sense of failure diving into her stomach instead. "Don't flatter yourself. It's not like I was trying to seduce you."

He grinned. "No matter what your intentions were, you're safe with me. Unlike you, I don't intend to follow in the footsteps of my own deadbeat dad."

Then, with a wry expression, Connor walked to the kitchen, causing Lacey to wonder what he'd meant by that last cryptic comment.

Chapter Four

Connor knew that his last statement had really gotten to Lacey.

As they'd cleaned the dining room and kitchen, she'd watched him with a speculative gleam in her gray-blue eyes. Not that he was about to explain what he'd meant by "I don't intend to follow in the footsteps of my own deadbeat dad."

Conn must have been gnashing his teeth or something equally obvious because, just as he and Lacey finished the last of the clean up, she cleared her throat, jolting him.

He pushed aside his thoughts and tried to grin at her. "Guess it's time to call it a night," he said.

"Yeah." Her eyes were huge, made more so by

her sophisticated hairdo. "I'm glad you could make it, what, between your cabin renovation and bird-watching."

"A man's got to eat."

She held up a finger. "There's caramel-covered flan for dessert, if you want it."

"You mean to trap me here with food, don't you?"

"A man's got to eat," she said, using his own ammunition against him.

Hell. Did he really want to go back to that cabin yet? Conn had never felt so isolated in his life. For a guy who'd grown up with a steady diet of family and friends, he was sadly lacking both lately. Besides, this woman's unconditional acceptance of him—no matter his identity—warmed him to the core. She was a rarity: openhearted, beautiful, unexpected.

Watch out, he thought.

"I know what you're going to say to dessert," Lacey said. "You've got to leave."

"No," he said. "Not yet, at least."

She perked up at that. "Great. Just give me a minute to dish the flan and—"

"But let's go for a change of scenery. Okay? On my way over here I noticed that the air's friendly, and it's a good night for—"

He cut himself off, thinking of past twilights sitting on the porch with Emily Webster, watching the sun as it changed angles over the manicured lawns of their hometown street. She'd always wanted to talk about wedding dresses or caterers during these reverent moments. He'd merely wanted to watch in silence. He wondered if Lacey would want to talk his ears off, too.

"It's a good night for just enjoying the peace of it," he finished.

She nodded, as if understanding. "You've had enough Spanish guitars, I suppose."

He didn't say a word, merely lifted a brow in response. She'd said it better than he could've anyway.

Later, after donning their heavy weather gear, both of them carried their desserts outside. Conn had been right, too. The hushed air was a blanket of moonlight, sweeping over the ground and its comforter of snow. Flakes sparkled in intervals, holding together the countryside with glittering stitches.

Lacey waved him away from the big house's floodlights, then trudged over to a dark, hidden nook, brushing off a stone bench with a gloved hand before inviting him to take a seat next to her.

As his eyes adjusted, Conn saw that they were sitting by what seemed to be a pagoda-lined Japanese stone garden.

The craggy silhouettes of three-foot stone lanterns and miniature bridges stood guard over snow-fluttered rocks and a pond. He could imagine the pooled ice melting to water in the springtime, offering relaxation, a place to escape.

"This rivals my front porch in Montana," he said, his voice lowered so as not to disturb the moment.

He heard a soft murmur from Lacey, an acknowledgment, really. Then that was that.

They just sat there for a while, poking at their custardlike dessert, neither of them actually eating anything.

Damn, he felt huge and out of place sitting next to her, camped among these miniature models of Japanese architecture.

Sliding a glance over to Lacey, he caught his breath. Moonlight breathed over her skin, smoothing over her cheek with the luminescent texture of a pearl necklace. She'd closed her eyes, a slight smile curving her lips.

"What's so amusing?" he asked. Damn the silence. It was killing him.

She laughed and opened her eyes, staring at the shadows of her rock garden. "Full circles," she said. "Everything comes full circle sometime or another."

"I'm not going to pretend I know what you're talking about."

Or did he?

She lifted up both her hands in a so-help-me gesture. "A long time ago, I lived somewhere that had a stone garden. I could put my head together there. I could be left alone to think. It's funny, but all I ever wanted to do was get out of that place with its garden. And I did. But look where I am now—in another pagoda-accessorized location just like it. One that I cultivated."

Her voice ended on a note of such wistfulness it

was all Conn could do to keep to himself. He wanted to put an arm around her shoulders, nestle her against him, offer comfort. It was only natural for him to reach out to people—he'd grown up in a house where hugs and touches were a part of life.

But here in Kane's Crossing, it was a bad idea.

"So this is full circle for you, huh?" he asked. "You're back where you started."

"Pretty much." She seemed to snap out of her daze, turning so she faced him. "Somehow I think you're doing the same thing. Don't ask me why."

He wouldn't. That was for damned sure. The fact that she could guess he was on his way to closing up the loose ends of his and his mother's lives was too uncomfortable to think about.

Was he that much of a simpleton? Was he that obvious, bumbling around the woods without much of a plan to confront the Spencers?

"Don't worry. I won't ask why you think I'm on some sort of mission," he said, putting a cap on the conversation.

She turned forward again, toward the garden. "Did you get much information during your bird-watching session today?"

She knew. Lacey Vedae knew what he was doing with those binoculars. Game over.

"Not much," he said.

A pause spanned the distance between them. "Listen, Connor. I don't know exactly what you're trying to accomplish in those woods, but I'll warn you about messing with the people who live in the Spencer mansion. You don't want to do it.''

Could he still get away with acting like he didn't know what she was talking about? Could he still be the innocuous country boy from Montana?

Worth a try. ''I don't mean to get involved in their business.''

He hoped the message held a double meaning for her.

''Do you have any idea what the Spencers are all about?'' she asked.

''You're a tenacious little devil.''

''That's not the half of it, you know. If you take it into your head to go around Kane's Crossing asking about that family, you'd best watch yourself. Half this town would go to war for them because that's the way it's always been. The Spencers have owned this town since the beginning, and some people don't want that to change.''

Now he was the one turning toward her, too interested to care how his body language was giving him away. ''How about the other half?''

''Oh, boy.'' Lacey shook her head. ''Now you're getting into some deep hurts, because the other half are my friends. The anti-Spencer brigade.''

Connor knew he would never find the information he needed to arm himself against the Spencers in some newspaper. He wanted firsthand dirt, straight from someone close to the source.

''What about it, Lacey?''

She stood, her Spanish-fringed hem brushing the snow as the wind picked up. Clouds had started to form in the distance, giving her posture a moody cast. She nodded toward the Spencer estate. "A lot of townsfolk thought the strife would end when Horatio and Edwina left Kane's Crossing."

Conn tried to contain the flash of fire that lit through his body at the mention of Horatio's name. "Are they gone for good?"

"I think so." Lacey clutched at her coat. "And Chad, their son, with them. Their troubles started when Nick Cassidy arrived in town. He had a beef with Chad, who'd framed Nick for a crime he didn't commit. Nick wanted some revenge and returned here to get it."

Conn balled his hands into fists. Seems his mother wasn't the only one who'd been worked over by the Spencers. "And?"

"And Nick ended up buying a lot of Spencer property and giving it to citizens who needed the money. He married Meg Thornton, too. People used to whisper that she'd gotten pregnant by Chad and given birth to his twins. I say it doesn't matter. Nick and Meg just had another little baby, a girl. Molly."

Even in the moonlight, Conn could see Lacey's hazy smile, could see it was touched with something more than happiness for the Cassidys.

Loneliness?

No. He couldn't care, couldn't get involved. "So

that's the reason the Spencers got the hell out of Dodge? Because of Nick Cassidy?''

"No, that was just the beginning. Chad had already gotten married and moved to Europe. Nick's actions were only enough to weaken Horatio Spencer, not destroy the family.

"That's when Sam Reno, Nick's foster brother, came back to town to take over the office of Sheriff. Sam uncovered crimes that the Spencers had committed in their toy factory, crimes that had killed Sam and Nick's father. The final nail in Horatio's coffin, though, was when Ashlyn, his daughter, helped Sam in his investigation.''

Ashlyn. He'd already read that she'd gone against the Spencers.

Would she be an ally?

"What happened to this Ashlyn?'' asked Conn, hoping he didn't sound too desperate for information. Newspapers had told him about some of these details, but Lacey was giving him more than he'd hoped for.

"She married Sam. You built a snow wookie with Taggert, their adopted son. Remember him?''

"Yeah,'' he said with a slight smile. "I remember.''

How could he forget the kid who'd dragged him out of the woods yesterday? Though Conn wasn't sure "dragged'' was the appropriate word.

He held the image of little Taggert for a second longer, packing the boy's energetic, cocky grin into another notch on his heart, where he could enjoy it later.

Lacey came to stand in front of him, cooling what must've been an absent grin on his face as her shadow angled over him. "Ashlyn is a good friend. I'd walk into the fires of hell for her."

Connor appreciated the sentiment. Not that he could tell that to this petite bulldog in front of him.

Instead of a "thank you," which is what he really wanted to express, he said, "I'm sure she'd do the same for a friend like you."

"The only reason I'm telling you this gossip is that I want you to have it straight. All right? You ask anyone else in this town and they'll give you some warped rendition of the truth. My friends deserve more than that."

Maybe she was about to say something else, but instead she clamped shut her mouth and merely stood there.

Connor took to his feet, hovering near her, thinking how fragile she seemed against the delicate pagoda shadows—shapes that looked as if they'd been torn from black paper and pasted against the snow.

"Thank you," he whispered, the words laden with more meaning than "thanks for dinner" or "thanks for the lesson in Kane's Crossing history."

She peered up at Conn, eyes muted by the shaded night, her thick eyelashes emphasizing how delicate she was next to someone like him.

"That's my problem," she said. "I suppose I'd walk through fire for anyone who deserved it."

Her words shot him through with admiration, drawing him to her once again. He found himself tracing a finger around her pouty mouth as he lost track of his heartbeat. Without thinking, he bent and pressed his lips to her forehead.

Thank you.

He lingered, consumed by the scent of her hair. Ethereal. A mix of rose petals, honey and tangerine. Soothing as sunlight warming his face, bringing a sense that all was right with the world.

When he lifted his head, he didn't move, frozen by what he'd done. He'd crossed a line in the snow, gone somewhere he couldn't return from. Through the tips of his fingers, he felt a shudder pass through her body, and the electricity made him shift, made him want to step back while yearning to move forward.

Confused, he moved his head slightly, and she gasped.

"Strange," she whispered. Lacey narrowed her eyes, breaking the moment with her unexpected comment. "The way the moonlight hit you. You remind me of…"

She shook her head and turned around, but he could still hear her mutter, "Don't even say it, Lacey."

"What?" he asked.

"Oh, boy. You'll think I'm batty." She glanced over her shoulder, gauging his reaction.

"I'll think you're being coy if you don't come out with it."

She grinned and turned back around. "You look like someone in that light. Jeez, it's probably just my imagination."

Now he was really curious. "And...?"

She paused, considering him. Then, with a flourish, she held out her hand. "The hour is late, the streets of Kane's Crossing are deserted... Do you want to see something uncanny?"

The town was empty. Damn, what the hell.

"I suppose I do," he said, folding Lacey's fingers into his own hand, trying not to concentrate on how lightheaded he got when she touched him.

"Then let's go." She tugged him along, away from the stone garden, away from the house.

Away from the woods.

It hadn't taken more than fifteen minutes to drive to Pioneer Square but, all the while, Lacey had been more than aware of Connor sitting in the passenger's seat of her sports car.

He'd had his lips on her forehead, for Heaven's sake. Yes, that mouth had been *touching* her. Ah, heavy sigh.

Lacey had almost shot straight up to the sky. Even now, reliving the warmth of his breath, the proximity of his body as it towered over her, she couldn't quite control her reaction.

And that worried her.

Didn't eighth-grade girls get all cross-eyed and starstruck at the thought of an innocent kiss? How embarrassing to realize she hadn't grown out of the roller-coaster-stomach stage of romance.

Heck, she might as well go home right now and doodle ''Connor + Lacey'' on the cover of a notebook while she was at it.

Don't dwell on it, she thought to herself, as she parked then led Connor through the softly howling wind, past the historic antebellum Willowbreeze House to the center of Pioneer Square. An old stone church rested on the other side of the park, as if watching over the latticed gazebo and the surrounding willow trees. The effect was eerie.

She brought him to the foot of a statue. ''Welcome to the hub of all social life in Kane's Crossing.''

Connor laughed. ''This? I expected maybe a bowling alley or a pool hall to be your pulpit of celebration.''

''We do have those, as well, in our rowdy little town. But once the weather clears here, the party begins.''

''You're being sarcastic.''

''Unfortunately, I'm not.''

The sky had clouded over, and soft drifts of snow floated over them. They melted over his tied-back hair, over his tanned skin. ''Why do you live here, Lacey? It's obviously not your kind of paradise.''

She'd asked herself the same question too many times. ''I found out a long time ago that I can't stand to be away from my family. I spent a long time moving from house to house with my mom, who couldn't seem to settle down with one man. When we found the Shanes—'' heat caught in her throat, but she gulped away the emotion ''—I knew I was home.''

By now the air was filled with snowflakes. They landed on her cheeks, on her lips. Lacey closed her eyes, tasting the moist chill of them. She didn't want Connor to see how much family meant to her.

They were everything.

''Family is the most important gift in the world.'' Connor's jaw clenched just before he turned away, absolutely unaware of how he'd echoed her thoughts.

''Yeah, well, tell that to my mom.'' She managed to laugh, but the gesture's cynicism didn't make her feel any better.

After a moment, Connor turned back to Lacey, drops of snow balancing on his eyelashes. She wanted to brush her cheek against them, feel the long, wet spikes bristle against her skin. She wanted to feel the heat of him against her.

''What about your mom?'' he asked gently.

She shrugged. No big deal, right? ''She's living in Vegas now, serving cocktails to some poor sucker who'll find himself in a marriage of her convenience.''

''You didn't want to stay with her?''

She thought of Rick, her cocky, protective stepbrother. Of Matt, her responsible older stepbrother. Of

Dad, who'd died and left her with enough comfort and security to last a lifetime.

"No, thanks." Darn, there was that burn in her throat again, making it impossible to form more words. She wanted to tell him it was okay that her mom had never known what to do with her. That it was okay she'd dumped her into HazyLawn to let the doctors deal with a severely depressed teenage daughter.

But when Lacey tried to talk again, all that came out was something close to a sob.

"Lacey?"

Through the splash of her tears she saw his boots, blurred and smudged under the lightly falling snow. "I'm fine. Just…"

A wave of melancholy overcame her. *Fight it, fight it. Don't let it control you, Lacey.*

"Hey." The boots made their way toward her, stopping near her own feet.

She felt Connor's hands on her shoulders, then his finger under her chin. When he tilted up her head to meet his gaze, a tremble tore through her.

He was looking into her, seeing all her shortcomings, every mortifying minute of her life:

Spacy Lacey…

Isn't your name really Lacey V.D., as in venereal disease?

Then came the laughter. The cruel, vindictive adolescent laughter that probably seemed so harmless to the other kids.

Lacey tried to avert her face, tugging away from his grasp. She couldn't let him see how much hurt was inside, how much pain was clawing to get out.

"I'm okay," she said, meaning to sound strong.

But she'd only whispered.

He took her face in his hands, cupping her jawline, using his fingertips to sketch every angle, every inch that had mocked her in the mirror as a teenager.

She'd hated that face, hated everything around her.

She repeated, "I'm okay," this time louder, as if she needed to convince herself of the words more than anyone else.

But her bravura couldn't cover the quake of her voice. The shaking traveled from her throat down her chest, consuming her heart, her belly, her legs.

She didn't know if she could gather enough breath to talk anymore.

A snowflake winged past her vision, matching the white flares in Connor's blue eyes, then settled on her lower lip. As it started to melt, he leaned in, touching his mouth to hers, tasting what was now water.

The precipitation made their kiss sleek and tender, and Lacey sighed, never having experienced a man who took enough time to touch her face as he pressed against her. Before, she'd only been pawed at by boys who hadn't grown up enough to be considered men, guys who'd merely kissed then told. Then there'd been one man who'd asked her to be with him, and she'd taken a chance. Then lost.

But now, with Connor sipping at her lips, with his

massive body blocking the light, Lacey knew what she'd won tonight.

Passion.

It beat through her like the thunder of a waterfall on rock. It made her want to burrow next to him, run her hands into the folds of his jacket to explore the breadth of his chest, the span of his shoulders. It made her want to lose control.

For the moment.

Because, as soon as he raised his lips from hers, the doubts mobbed back, poking her in the ribs like wayward children with pencils, reminding her that Connor would just be another guy who'd get that look in his eyes—that scared witless look—when he found out about her battle with depression.

They broke apart, and Lacey touched her fingertips to her mouth, feeling her lips throb with the aftermath of his warmth.

Connor glanced at the ground, shook his head. "That was ill advised, huh?"

Exactly. He was already regretting it.

"My lips were cold anyway," she said, trying to make light of the situation. She had to say something, anything, to relieve the tension. "I didn't bring us out here to freeze to death."

"Right." He shoved his hands in his jacket, peering around Pioneer Square. "What's this uncanniness you wanted me to see?"

God, he'd kissed her. Kissed *her*. What had he been thinking?

But maybe he had the right idea. Maybe pretending as if the kiss hadn't happened would make life much easier in the long run.

She cleared her throat, steadying herself, then gestured to the statue. "I was getting around to showing you. Look up here."

He did, and after a second his jaw muscles twitched, his body tensed. "This is some kind of joke."

"I don't think so." Lacey glanced at him, long and hard. Same bone structure, same mouth...

"Who is it?" asked Connor.

But Lacey had a feeling he knew the answer. Heck. The whole town would know the answer once he showed his face in public.

"It's our esteemed Kane Spencer, town founder. And you're the spitting image of him."

He tore his gaze away from the statue to her. She could've sworn that there was a wary note in the way he didn't comment.

The snowfall increased, hammering at them, biting at their skin with the renewed force of its descent.

"So," she said, her voice gaining strength. "Why is it that you two could be twins?"

Chapter Five

Instead of responding, Conn headed for the car, the snow zooming around him like so many unanswered questions.

Behind him, Lacey's voice rushed to catch up. "Connor? Come on. You're not going to be able to keep this a secret."

He waited for her on the driver's side of the vehicle, opening the door for her once she appeared. Silent, he waited until she climbed inside, then shut the door and settled himself in the cab.

Wind rattled the windows, flakes skydiving past his view. What could he say to her without blowing his purpose for being in Kane's Crossing?

Hello, I'm your friendly neighborhood bastard, and

I've come to claim my place in the family who's wreaked havoc on your town for the past few decades. The family who's trying to crash your glass castle.

"Connor…"

"Lacey." He kept his eyes on the dashboard, on the suicidal snowflakes crashing against the windshield. "I've got nothing to say on the subject except that it's a coincidence. Nothing but that."

"Are you related to the Spencers?"

Connor held up the hand nearest to her, as if he could stop the interrogation merely by blocking it with a palm.

Next to him, Lacey sat silently, probably thinking of who to tell the news to first: his half sister, Ashlyn?

A sister, he thought with wonder.

He'd always wanted one of those, but his mother had given birth to only a single child. Connor, the secret she'd kept for years.

He lowered his hand, the reality of a family—a sister, a nephew named Taggert, too—getting to him. "I need time."

More silence.

He continued. "I understand your curiosity, but if you choose to talk about me to anyone in this town, it'll cause more damage than good."

Conn could almost read her mind. *Who are you?*

The unspoken question echoed through the car, made all the worse because he didn't know the answer.

Why couldn't he tell Lacey about his mother, her

weakened body attacked by a cancer that had invaded her liver and spread to other parts of her body? Why couldn't he tell her about his greatest fear: that his mom would fall out of remission and die because they couldn't afford the cost of treatment?

At the very least, he could reveal that he needed to confront the Spencers because they had the means to save the life of a woman who'd given birth to one of their own. Right? Couldn't he do that?

Wind moaned over the car, tracing the streamlined curves with cold, uncaring fingers of sound.

Conn didn't trust Lacey with the truth. Not yet.

He heard her weary sigh, saw the slump of her shoulders out of the corner of his eye when she reached for the ignition.

As she started the engine, the roar cut between them with a jagged finality.

The next day, in her Louisville office, Lacey couldn't concentrate on the work at hand.

She leaned back in her padded leather swivel chair and stared at the expansive plateau of her walnut desk. Memos, reports, neatly stacked manila folders and her laptop computer stared back at her, waiting to be closed out for the day. Brass accents gleamed under the bright lights of her office, reminding her that this was still a man's domain, a lair where her stepfather used to work; this is where he'd driven himself to an early grave. Matt used to spend too much time here as well—so much it'd almost ruined his marriage to Rachel.

Lacey knew how to balance work and home. She ran a tight ship at Shane Industries, with its main product of horse feed and supplies. But what if she burned out and failed, just as some of the older employees expected her to?

Lacey shook her head and clicked out of her laptop's e-mail program. As usual, she'd taken quick care of all her meetings today, had troubleshot some product delivery issues and handled a couple of labor gripes. Her dad had always possessed such confidence in her work ethic, in her efficiency and enthusiasm, and his positive support had molded her success, forced her to work that much harder so she wouldn't let down the Shane name.

Everything about her life was wonderful. So why was a bite of negativity nibbling at her today?

She stood, wandering past the Renoir prints she'd picked out to "feminize" the office space, wandering past the various ferns and potted plants that brought some life into the dark wood of this so-called "man's world."

When she came to the window, she stopped, staring at the city below, unable to keep her mind from wandering.

Where had Connor gone after they'd gotten home last night?

She shouldn't have been so nosy, shouldn't have pushed him so far with her questions. Sure, it was obvious he wanted something from the Spencers. It was equally clear he could've passed for one of the family, as well, which got her to thinking...

Oh, please, Lacey, she told herself. Your imagination is working overtime again. Chances are that Connor Langley is *not* a Spencer, so go back to your paper shuffling and corporate whip-wielding and mind your own business.

A low voice pushed into her thoughts. "Looks like you're ready to fly, Your Bossiness."

She turned away from the window to face her step-brother and pilot, Rick. A newlywed, Rick never failed to impress Lacey with the way he'd made such a turnaround in his life the past couple of months. Where he used to resemble a bleeding shadow, with his dark brown hair and bottomless eyes, he now smiled as if he meant it, though he still had a taste for black-rebel clothing.

"Eager to get home to Daisy?" asked Lacey, referring to Rick's wife.

"As always." He leaned against the door frame, laconically crossing his arms over his chest. "Ready to sit on the therapist's couch? The town car's outside."

"I'm ready." To what? To tell Dr. Franco that the Prozac was working fine, no side effects, no major melancholy, except for last night's slip? That she hadn't relapsed in the six months since her last depressive episode and the start of her medication? Or should she talk about Connor and how he was stirring her up, making her wonder if he was that one man who wouldn't care about her past, her dark struggles?

Lacey returned to her desk to shut down her laptop and stuff papers in her shoulder-strap briefcase. "I'm deciding what to work on at home. Could you fly me here again in a couple of days? I've set up a meeting with some distributors."

"Sure thing." Rick still stared at her, as if she was avoiding the real topic. Which she was, of course.

Out of all the people in the world, he knew her the best. In fact, he'd been one of the keys to her victory over depression. After her mother had married Russell Shane, Lacey had finally found a family who supported her, understood her, let her know that life was a chain of possibilities and not a stagnant pool of resignation.

"Really, Rick." Lacey packed up her computer, then slung that and her briefcase over her shoulder. "I'm fine."

He nodded. "If you say so. It's just that you seem…preoccupied."

"I'm phasing out of corporate mode. Give me another minute and I'll be back to the normal Lacey Vedae."

"Does your mood have anything to do with the smoke I saw coming from the old cabin?"

Adrenaline jolted—cold as an icicle stab—through Lacey's chest. "Smoke?"

"Living on the other side of the woods gives me an excuse to watch over you. Remember? Daisy and

I smelled smoke last night after we got home from our weekend getaway.''

''Oh, *smoke*.'' Lacey managed to laugh, thinking at the same time that she'd have to tell Connor to stop using the fireplace. Didn't she have a space heater he could have instead? ''Right. It was those teenagers again, playing house. I shooed them out of the cabin before they could set the place aflame.''

Rick unfolded his posture from the door frame. ''I don't like you running after those kids, Lace. You call me or Sheriff Reno before you go out there. Understand?''

''Are you ordering me around?''

''Damn straight.''

''You're my big brother, not my sovereign.''

''Lacey.'' He was giving her that don't-mess-with-me expression.

''Rick,'' she answered in the same chiding tone.

''Hey, I don't want my little sis getting damaged. All right?''

Lacey started to whisk past him, out of the office. ''You're far too protective. Besides, that cabin is on my list of to-do's. I've hired a handyman to fix it up. So don't get worried about signs of life out there.''

Boy, she hoped he'd buy the handyman line.

Even as she said it, she knew Rick would take the warning comments in stride. He'd spent too much time when they were younger defending her in fights when the kids would say mean things, when the girls would corner her in the school bathrooms and screech rumors into her face. Matt had done his share of fist-a-cuffing, too, though he'd gone off to college during the worst of it, leaving Rick to carry the burden of being "big brother."

Lacey checked out with her administrative assistant, then she and Rick took the elevator to the lobby. From there, a company car waited to drive them to her doctor's office, then to the airport where Rick's Cessna would take them home.

As they both climbed into the back seat, Rick reached out to tweak her chin.

"What's this with the fancy hair and frilly skirt?" he asked.

"Technically, I'm wearing a chignon. I've got some Spanish flair going."

"I like it, even if your mom would pitch a fit at your new runway style."

Yeah, Lacey cared. "My mom's in some two-bit casino balancing martinis and cheap champagne on a tray while traipsing around in three-inch heels. You want to talk fashion victim?"

The words held a hint of bitterness. To erase the aftertaste, Lacey shrugged as if the thought didn't matter.

"It's in the past," said Rick. "Don't worry about it."

Okay, don't worry about it. No sweat. Forget that her mom had hated the way Lacey dressed from the first time she'd walked out of her room in grade school, wearing what she thought was a nice take on

Cyndi Lauper cool. Teased out hair with a sheer scarf spiking out from her tresses, a loud-pink tube top, a frilly paisley skirt and combat boots. Lacey had thought she was *it*. MTV beauteous.

When Carrie Vedae Smithstone Shane had gotten a load of her daughter, she'd commanded Lacey to march right back to her closet to wear something decent. Uh-huh. As decent as her mom's busty necklines and knee-high ''love me, baby'' boots?

Lacey had gone back into her room, all right. And she'd come right back out with one of her poem books, camping out on her parent's bed while good old Mom had teased her own hair and applied a coat of makeup to her face. For the next five minutes, Lacey had read her a ditty about how it was okay to dress in your own style.

Russell—her beloved stepdad—had bought her this book in an effort to encourage individuality in his stepdaughter. Carrie had just as easily snatched it out of Lacey's hands and thrown it in a wastebasket.

''I don't know what to do with you,'' her mother had said, right before taking Lacey by one of her lace-gloved hands and leading her to the clothes closet.

There, Mommy Dearest had tossed out most of Lacey's garments, pointing out all the suitable outfits she had to wear.

Unfortunately, Lacey had chosen this time to learn to talk back. And it had cost her.

Carrie Vedae Smithstone Shane had locked Lacey

in that closet for an hour, the outside knobs tied with the scarf tugged out of Lacey's Cyndi Lauper hair.

But it was all fine in the end. Locking Lacey in a walk-in closet had been like setting a female loose in a chocolate factory. She'd spent the time trying on different fashion combinations, amusing herself by dressing like Prince and Madonna.

Rick had finally gotten her out of the makeshift prison, only to have Lacey's mother cry and apologize as she always did after doing something awful. Something like going on a drinking binge or withdrawing into a soap-opera-watching stupor and ignoring the kids.

She'd given Lacey so many things: life, challenges, a new family to love. And the depression gene, too.

Lord knew why Lacey's stepdad had married Carrie. Probably because she was young, usually full of energy and pretty in a prealcoholic way. After Russell's death, Carrie hadn't retained her looks. She'd gone back to Vegas to hunt for Lacey's real dad—never finding him—while Lacey had stayed in Kane's Crossing, her stepfather's daughter to the end.

"I miss him," Lacey said, a wistful twist to her voice.

Rick stiffened, then put an arm around her shoulders. "Me, too, Lace."

Maybe she shouldn't have said anything. Rick and Dad had struggled through a strained relationship at best, and Rick regretted the fact that they'd been at odds when Dad had died.

Couldn't she have left well enough alone? "I'm sorry," she said.

"Hey, little sis, forget it."

The tires whizzed over the dusk-lit streets on their way to the therapist, underlining the silence.

Ultimately, following a run-of-the-mill chat with Dr. Franco in which Lacey decided to keep Connor all to herself for now, Rick and she didn't say anything of substance. Not until Rick had flown them through clear skies back to Lexington and they were ensconced in his Jeep, on their way back to Kane's Crossing.

As Rick pulled up in Lacey's driveway, he glanced toward the woods. "You'll be okay?"

"Absolutely." Lacey pecked her stepbrother on the cheek. "Don't even think twice about me."

"Then Daisy and I will see you soon? Matt wants to get together, you know, to make up for all that lost time he was a jerk to us."

Matt. She was thankful that having him as a brother was easier now that his amnesia had disappeared.

"I'll be there," she said, lifting her hand in a slow wave before shutting the door and watching Rick drive away.

House lights ushered her to the warmth of the foyer, where a trace of last night's Spanish spices still lingered in the air. She wondered if Connor had been using his binoculars again today, wondered if he was still sore at her for not minding her own life.

She went about the business of preparing a quick

dinner—pasta with a sun-dried tomato alfredo sauce—all the while glancing at the woods. She must've gotten lost in her thoughts, because a sharp rap at the kitchen door startled her.

Was it The Wanderer again?

The shadow against the glass revealed a much larger figure.

Connor.

The breath left her, heating her with anticipation. But she managed to collect herself, then answered the summons.

He had his hat in hands, his hair unbound and spread over his shoulders like strands of sunlight. "Evenin', Lacey."

"Hello."

He worked the hat through his fingers, spinning it slowly while tracing the rim. "I was rude again last night, wasn't I?"

"You don't answer to me." The truth of her comment made her feel ashamed. He'd obviously felt guilty enough to tramp through day-old snow to perform an apology.

"I guess I don't. Still, I want to smooth things out between us." He paused, grinned sheepishly. "You had a long day of work. I had to wait the whole time through in order to apologize. It was hell on my pride."

Lacey froze. She wouldn't tell him about her therapy appointment. If he knew, he'd turn his back on her, and she couldn't bear the thought of his negative opinion. Even imagining the horror on his face was awful enough.

She *couldn't* tell him. Not if she wanted him to look at her without prejudice.

He broke into her thoughts, softly saying, "I've come to ask for something."

She stopped staring at his hat and met his eyes—his deep blue, starburst eyes. "Yeah?"

He hesitated again, seeming to Lacey like a man who stood at the edge of a cliff, taking a deep breath before stepping off the ledge.

"Will you take me to that glass castle of yours?" he asked. "Then I'll explain."

She smiled, relieved, all too happy to have avoided the secret of her shortcomings.

"See look, that's the Locksley castle!" said Lacey as they drove the long way to her dream project.

She pointed to the top of a distant hill at what looked like the shape of a mammoth compound, with tall stone barriers surrounding a—yes, it was—a castle. Turret-crowned towers peeked over the walls, making Connor wonder if the place had a bailey, moat and chapel besides.

"You've got to be kidding," he said, more to himself than anyone else.

"Oh, no." She sparkled with humor, with the flush of winter air pinking her cheeks. "Something's hidden up there. But you can't get past the iron gates that block a long drive up the hill. There're guards in blue uniforms who man the boundaries. Yup, something's happening up there, all right.''

"Has anyone ever tried to sneak past the sentries?''

As they turned a corner on the country road, the castle became a dark speck against the sky.

"Everyone has,'' she said. "The journey is almost a rite-of-passage in this place. Some kids say that it's empty, not even worth going to. Some kids say that someone's living there. I don't know what to believe.''

Connor lost sight of the castle and slumped in his seat, watching the winter landscape rush by the car windows. He was all out of the power to believe, himself.

This morning, he'd whipped the white tarp off the Chevy truck he'd parked behind the cabin and traveled to Lexington. There, he'd used yet another pay phone to check with his aunt about his mother's health, as he did every couple of days in some distant location.

She was holding steady, Aunt Trudy had said. It's too bad her son had to go driving off to Kane's Crossing on a fool's errand instead of seeing to his mother here in Raintree.

The accusation had hit home. He didn't want to be here. Didn't want to be chasing down a dream that probably wouldn't materialize.

When he'd talked to his mother on the phone, heard her weary, scraped voice over the line, he'd almost hopped in his truck and driven straight back to Montana. But she'd encouraged him to continue, to ignore Aunt Trudy's old-woman guilt trips.

You do what you think is right, she reminded him. *A boy should meet his dad, anyway, even if his errand* is *to ask for pity money.*

God, to meet his father. Yes, he did want to. But the desire disgusted him, made him feel disloyal to the good man who'd raised him as his own son.

"We're here," said Lacey, yanking the car's parking brake and cutting the engine.

They'd pulled up to a massive, stone warehouse. In a way, the granite resembled a castle's walls, blocking something mysterious and valuable beyond its guard.

As Lacey and he walked to the door to unlock it, she turned to him, her smile dazzling. "It's not completely done yet, obviously, but—"

She was making excuses, probably because of that whole "You'll think I'm crazy for doing this" thing she'd mentioned the night she'd first brought the endeavor up.

He didn't reveal that he wasn't much interested in the castle itself. He wanted to get a feel for the property, for the reason the Spencers wanted this land back. He wanted ammunition. The lawyers he'd seen today in Lexington had started their own research into the Spencers' holdings, and Connor thought it would be wise to do his part, too.

"Just open the door, Lacey," he said, trying not to sound overly impatient.

That silly grin lit her face as she yanked open the sliding door, the wheels on their tracks roaring like a roll of fire.

Darkness, except for a presence, an expectation hanging in the air.

Then Lacey hit the lights, and Connor couldn't stop himself from flinching at the sight before him:

Parapet walks circling towers that spiraled toward the air with cut-crystal strength; stairs inside of those towers, leading toward gold-etched machicolation where phantom warriors could hide and shoot arrows at fantasy dragons; banners, flying in the same gold-stiff glory, catching the winds of a young woman's dream.

"Good God, Lacey. This has to cost a fortune."

She barely moved in a shrug, seemingly too busy in gauging his reaction to respond. "It's everything I own."

Rainbow-arched light refracted from an overhead lamp, casting a wealth of colors over Lacey's skin. Connor wanted to wrap his fingers around that spectrum, to grasp something that didn't actually exist and put it in his pocket.

Lacey sighed and became all business. She gestured toward unpolished materials and shapes. "The workers are putting the final touches on the rampart and a drawbridge. And they're thinking of using real water for a moat. I'm still mulling over that idea."

"No." Connor stepped nearer, still stunned by the

utter scope of Lacey's ambition. "Leave the moat glass. Has your family seen this?"

"Sure." Lacey laughed. "They think I've gone off the deep end. But they're still one hundred percent behind this, especially because of its ties to the Reno Center."

He realized this charitable project would make or break Lacey. Her giving nature tore at him, ripping at his skin to reveal the respect beneath it. "I think you're right," he said, extending some confidence. "People will come to this, just to stare. Just to know it's possible."

Lacey shrugged, as if she really didn't care.

"Damn them all anyway," she said.

"Damn who?"

"Oh…" She walked nearer the castle, and the rainbow disappeared from her cheeks. "All the people who ever doubted me. 'She's putting *what* in the old toy warehouse? That place is for storin' stuffed animals, not for buildin' glass castles.' Hah. I'm going to watch every face when they come in here opening day. I'm going to do some gloating."

There was a definite cut to her voice. "People can have big mouths. They don't think about what they say."

"Tell me about it." She smiled at him. "So, Connor Langley. On a scale of one to ten, how nutso am I? Or do I zing right off the charts?"

He wondered if he could get away with using "brilliant" as a euphemism for "nutso."

His legs were clearly doing a worse job of thinking than he was. He found himself next to her, yet again. Found himself avoiding his original reason for being here.

Who wanted to check out the land and the structures when something much more intriguing was staring you in the face?

His jacket brushed hers, and the whisping sound of the contact melted over the skin of his lower belly, tightening it. "You're a visionary."

"I like that terminology," she said, giving him a satisfied nod.

"Maybe one day I'll also find the bravery to turn what's inside of me into a reality."

An excess of information. He knew it, too. But this time, Lacey didn't beat him over the head with more questions. She merely kept staring at her creation, as if enamored of it. Scared of it.

He was afraid, as well. Afraid of pursuing a family he didn't know. Fearful of the betrayal he'd no doubt feel when he knocked on the Spencers' door to announce his existence. He'd be turning away from John Langley, his adoptive father, the man who'd given him his name and unconditional love. When John—it was odd to think of him as Dad now—had fallen off a roof while repairing it and died, Connor had vowed to keep his family safe, just as John would have.

What would the man have thought of Connor now? Did it matter? His mother didn't deserve to waste away from cancer when the Spencers owed her something. And that something could pay for a cure. Connor was sure of it.

They owed his family for her degradation. Especially since Horatio—his biological father—had known damn well that Connor existed.

Lacey was watching him. Good God, he probably had every emotion flitting over his face—butterflies of empty feeling, as colorful as glass-castle rainbows.

As he met her gaze, he pushed back a sense of growing hunger, a need to touch another person who understood what he was going through. Another person who was turning her dreams into something solid.

''One of these days,'' she said, ''when I know what you're all about, Connor Langley, I'll be able to say without qualification that you *are* brave. I'm sure you'll match my expectations.''

The innocence of her words slashed at him, sawing through his skin with a steel-tipped bite. Little did she know that he might be the dragon outside her castle.

Little did she know what being a Spencer meant.

Chapter Six

As the days passed, Conn actually started to look forward to Lacey's visits while he worked on the cabin's roof. Even if she was preoccupied with Shane Industries and last-minute castle preparations, she always found enough endearing energy to lecture him about using a space heater instead of the fireplace. Most importantly, she kept him up on town gossip, and that's how he found out about the town meeting in Kane Spencer Hall.

Intrigued, Conn decided he'd attend, even if Lacey didn't.

Big mistake, walking into this place by himself. Into this den of murmuring sharp tongues, punch bowls filled to the brim with the high school's home ec club poison of the week. Jammed with starch-collared citizens and dirt-jeaned farmers perched on their fold-out chairs while they waited for the meeting to begin.

Conn cursed to himself and inserted his body into the nearest dark corner, adjusting his hat over his brow so no one would notice him.

Hadn't Lacey told him he looked like Kane Spencer's statue? He'd best remember to cover his face.

What was he doing here anyway? Lacey had mentioned they'd be talking about "town matters," and his ears had perked up. He thought that while waiting for his lawyers to get back to him regarding the legality of his claim as an heir of the Spencer family, he'd best lay low.

Though he'd never told Lacey outright he was a Spencer, he knew she suspected it. These past few days, while they'd spent time together at what he now thought of as "his cabin" and her Japanese stone garden, they'd talked around the fact, and that was that, thank goodness.

A man with walruslike facial hair strutted to the front of the room, where a panel of townsfolk sat at a table, facing the crowd.

Conn had the feeling this was the town council, with their self-important postures and bureaucratic smiles. When he took a better look at them, he noticed one seat at the center of the table was conspicuously empty.

The swoop-mustached man banged a gavel on a

lectern, quieting the citizens. "I call to order this session of our town meeting. I, Mayor Dickens Strevels, shall preside."

As the mayor droned on, Conn settled back, trying to get comfortable against the wall. This place was foreign to him—as if he were a character in a colored motion picture who'd wandered into a black-and-white movie.

People in Raintree, Montana, didn't have names like Dickens, for Heaven's sake. Conn didn't think he belonged in a town where the possibility even existed.

As the council commenced its business, Conn found his attention wandering, his gaze combing the entrances for any sign of Lacey, scuttling into the meeting late, out of breath, her cheeks aglow from the nippy weather and an excess of enthusiasm.

Funny how things seemed a little boring without her here. He liked the way Lacey seemed to find a glass castle in every plain window of opportunity, how she saw him as Connor Langley—a guy he missed almost desperately.

Conn shook himself, digging his fingernails into his palm to stay alert, to keep his mind where it should be.

And it sure as hell shouldn't be on Lacey Vedae.

The meeting dragged on, featuring subjects that had nothing to do with the Spencers, nothing to do with Conn's interest in them. Topics ranging from what to do about the teenagers cruising in their cars from the Mom and Pop gas station on the edge of town to the bowling alley, to how to solve a dispute between two spinster women neighbors arguing about who owned a cat they both claimed.

In the middle of a debate regarding the delinquent removal of Christmas lights from a Main Street boutique, the room suddenly quieted.

A man with the sturdiness and majesty of a marble column marched down the middle aisle toward the front. His black coat flapped behind him, capelike. As he moved past the townsfolk, the people bowed their heads, peering at the new arrival from under their lowered brows.

The mayor even sent a stoic nod to the man. "Evening, Mr. Spencer."

Johann Spencer.

In his dark corner, Conn straightened, dipping down the brim of his hat so it all but covered his eyes.

Johann swept past the mayor. "I am running late tonight, Dickens." Then he took his seat in the center of the town council table.

The meeting took on a different tone, as if every word from here on out would be worth its weight in gold. As if each comment might mark a reputation for better or worse.

Johann seized a paper in front of his seat, then dismissed it by allowing it to float away from his long-fingered grasp. "Have we taken care of these matters on the agenda?"

He spoke with a slight accent, a cultured European

one. Even though Conn hadn't ever exchanged a word with the man, he bristled at the impersonality of his actions. Maybe cat ownership and Christmas decorations in late January were important to these townspeople whom Johann considered to be peons.

Or maybe Conn was angry because of the tiny spark of ambition that had started burning in his gut, a flare that said he was a Spencer—that he, too, could have people looking at him like he was the end-all-be-all. A fire that told him that he could have enough power to stop his mom from dying.

Was he actually jealous of Johann Spencer?

Inconceivable.

Mayor Strevels backed away from the lectern, tacitly gifting his leadership to Johann "Yes, Mr. Spencer. We've addressed those issues."

"Excellent." Johann steepled his hands on top of the table. "Last time we met, nothing was resolved in the case of Ms. Vedae and her claim to my family's land. I would like to discuss the situation."

Now Conn was all ears.

Johann paused, scanning the quiet crowd, his golden hair glinting under the town hall's bright lights. Hair so much like Connor's.

"I want her off that land," Johann said.

Mayor Strevels and a couple council members "harrumphed," apparently gathering up every ounce of courage in their bodies. The mayor spoke. "I'm afraid, Mr. Spencer, that her purchase was perfectly legal. It's not the duty of the town council to interfere in this private matter.''

Coolly, with the ease of a god flicking lightning across the sky for amusement, Johann said, ''Nick Cassidy and his legacy are the problem of everyone, *Dickens*.'' Zing. ''You recall that the man stole property from my blood. We only want what is rightfully ours.''

A councilman's face grew ruddy. ''With all due respect, Horatio Spencer left the country and—''

''—And Nick Cassidy is winning his vengeful crusade against the Spencers, even now.'' Johann sat back in his chair. ''It will not be tolerated.''

Connor's mind whirred. Was it possible the Spencers weren't what he'd thought? That they were trying to yank Lacey's land from under her castle because they were broke and grasping at straws?

Mom, he thought. *What other way is there to help you besides this hackneyed plan of mine? What else can I do?*

Johann continued. ''Scum like Cassidy should be cleared out from Kane's Crossing. He and his family are like trash after a big parade—useless clutter, stinking up our streets. Every month seems to bring in the curse of a new relative or friend. Sam Reno, our sheriff, whom the council somehow deemed qualified to keep watch over this town, for one. Lacey Vedae, for another. These people have no respect for town traditions or honor.''

Or maybe it wasn't about money.

Maybe Johann wanted that land back because of Spencer pride.

Either way, if he said another damned word about Lacey, Connor was going to lose it.

By now, several townsfolk had started clapping their hands, and it occurred to Conn that Lacey hadn't attended the meeting because it would be filled with people who hated her and her friends. Hadn't she tried to tell him about the ugly split in Kane's Crossing loyalties?

An elderly woman with salt-and-pepper hair popped out of her folding chair like a wiry Jack-in-the-Box, slashed smile and all. "They've been begging for some comeuppance ever since Nick Cassidy blinded people with his money. I know I speak for all the citizens when I say that we support you, Mr. Spencer!"

More applause. Connor noted the people—including most council members—who kept still, arms crossed. There were more than a few.

"Thank you, Mrs. Spindlebund," said Johann. "I have consulted my lawyers about the fraudulent land deal, but more importantly, I require the support of you, the good people of Kane's Crossing. Why do we need a glass castle in the old toy warehouse of *my family?*"

"True," echoed some voices.

Conn couldn't help being drawn and repelled by Johann's control. It was almost as if the world spun around his axis.

Why couldn't he command circumstances with his own mom? One woman, one problem, and Conn couldn't even handle *that* with any authority. The thought that he needed this man's help made him sick.

At this point, the mayor had taken a seat in the front row, slumped and defeated. However, Johann was evidently feeding off his supporters' gathering energy. He stood, towering over all the other council members, who merely watched in seeming timidity.

"Do we really want the cars of strangers speeding down our roads, endangering our children, on their way to see this monstrosity? Do we want the image of our town blighted by some crazy scheme from a women who has less than a sparkling reputation herself?"

Mrs. Spindlebund spoke up again. "My Sissy went to school with Lacey Vedae. They called her 'V.D.,' you know. One must wonder why that is."

Good God. The comment slapped Conn from the inside out, as if he had been insulted himself. Without even thinking, he stepped forward, unable to countenance this talk about Lacey, needing—for better or worse—to stand up for her.

"Hold it for a second," he said, his voice echoing right up to the high rafters.

A wave of human bodies turned tide to face him, every face a blank slate. No wonder, with his hat pulled over his eyes, with his coat probably making him seem like a brown bear who'd stumbled right out of the woods without a lesson in couth or common sense.

That's right. He had their attention. He just didn't know what the hell to say now.

As silence slid over him, every second making him feel more foolish than the previous one, Conn realized Johann was *seeing* him. No more hiding, trying to keep himself a secret.

A patronizing laugh drilled its way through Connor's thoughts, and he looked to the front of the room, to Johann, who was chuckling as if being entertained by his fool.

"Do you have something to add?" he asked Connor.

The man was addressing him, acknowledging his existence. Conn had imagined this moment many times as he'd peered through his binoculars at the Spencer estate. But the confrontation had been so much more dignified in his mind's eye. He'd been the one questioning, making demands.

The guy was leading a make-fun-of-Lacey session, dammit. Say your piece.

"Yeah, I've got something to add." Connor stepped forward again, so he could take advantage of the same light that shone upon Johann's head.

He slid off his hat with all the cool his relative would've used, then raised his head to the crowd.

For a moment, no one moved.

Or breathed.

After what seemed like an eon, the old woman, Mrs. Spindlebund, muttered, "Kane Spencer."

Conn allowed the name to circle the room while meeting the glance of every person who hadn't applauded during Johann's grandstanding. Then he met the stunned gaze of his own relative.

His Spencer kin.

He spoke. "It'd be ideal if Ms. Vedae were here to speak for herself, but that isn't the case. How you people can sit here and badmouth her is beyond me."

A few heads bowed in apparent shame. A few faces still stared in his direction, slack-jawed, uncomprehending.

Good.

Let them wonder. Let them sweat, guessing about the reason he looked so much like Kane Spencer.

"You all might want to get to know Ms. Vedae." Conn made eye contact with Johann again. "She's a good woman."

"Says whom?" said the other man, recovering, a smile cutting across his mouth.

Conn couldn't help his own grin from surfacing. Who had the power right now?

He might as well enjoy this moment while it lasted.

Taking his time, he positioned the hat back on his head and drew the rim over his eyes once again.

"Says someone who knows Ms. Vedae."

And, with that, he sauntered out of the room, aware of all the gazes trailing after him.

Aware that he'd said too damned much.

* * *

"You did what?" Lacey asked.

She could only stare as Connor leaned on her kitchen counter, a bottle of beer clasped in his hand. He'd shed his coat two footsteps past the threshold, leaving her to mentally sigh over that homespun shirt and how it was tucked so carelessly into the waistband of his tan pants. "I went to the town meeting tonight."

"But...why?"

Lacey didn't pause for an answer, since the question was rhetorical anyway. Connor would give her some line about wanting to take in the local color— or some such garbage neither of them would believe. Besides, she'd spent all day in her home office, trying to untangle sales figures for Shane Industries, then going over details for the opening of the glass castle in one week. She was in no mood to do more work.

Instead, she held up a hand, signaling she didn't want to know why he'd ventured into the big bad town of Kane's Crossing. Then she grabbed her full glass of late harvest Riesling—something, anything to relax her—and removed herself to the couch in front of the blazing fireplace.

She cuddled into the overstuffed cushions. "Actually, I don't want to know, Connor."

He followed suit, tentatively taking a spot on the opposite end of the couch. He probably was having another male reaction to the soothing music she'd put on the CD player. Beethoven's "Pastoral Symphony''—redolent of flowers, flowing sun dresses and fields of grass.

Connor said, ''I'm sure the meeting was no different than usual, so it wouldn't interest you anyway. It's what *I* want to know that's eating away at me.''

''Isn't that always the case?''

He flinched, as if she'd slapped his cheek and he was trying his best to be polite about it.

''Sorry,'' she said, gaze trained on the fire. The flames lulled her, calmed her. ''Bad day at the office. Go ahead. What do you want to know?''

No response. When she glanced at him, he was checking out her red silk robe. For a naughty moment, she even hoped that he was wondering what she was wearing beneath it.

Just some silky undies, she thought, fighting a grin.

His interest pumped up her heartbeat, crested the tips of her breasts until they tingled. She wished he'd just reach out and take one of them in a palm, run the tips of his fingers over it, chase away the ache.

Lacey crossed her arms over her chest, still holding her wine glass, hiding the evidence of her wayward thoughts.

The gesture seemed to break him out of his reverie. ''Before that meeting, I never realized how people in this town treat you.''

''What? Were they tossing around some insults as usual?'' Lacey tilted the wineglass to her lips, took a long swallow, hoped it'd obliterate the sour taste from her mouth. "And you wonder why I don't go to those things."

What if they said something about her stay in HazyLawn? What if they mentioned that she'd checked into the clinic her freshman year of high school? She took another sip of the Riesling.

Connor did likewise with his beer. Then, "A lady said you had V.D."

Lacey almost spit out the wine. "What?"

Connor laughed, maybe with some amount of relief. "Yeah. She said her daughter used to tease you about it in high school. Are you okay?"

"Jeez, Connor, if you're asking if I have a venereal disease, the answer is a resounding 'no.' I don't…I mean, there's no possible way."

Right. It was really easy for twenty-seven-year-old once-removed virgins to get syphilis or gonorrhea. Catching a case of social ostracism because of her lack of a sex life was far more likely. Besides, when she'd been with the one serious man in her life, they'd used a condom. But too bad they didn't make protection for the emotional side of lovemaking, as well.

"Anyway," she added, "that was just Sissy Spindlebund shooting off her mouth way back when the bitter rantings of cheerleaders mattered to me. I couldn't care less now."

Something inside her laughed at that. Something old, tucked back. Something she'd chased away with the help of HazyLawn and the Shane family.

When she glanced at Connor, the corners of his

mouth were turned down, his eyes a sad shade of blue. Sympathy.

"Hey," she said, "I don't need you to accompany me on the world's smallest violin. School was a nightmare, sure. Isn't it that way for everyone?"

"No."

"Oh, of course. You lived in Raintree—Simpleville, U.S.A., right?"

Connor's answering chuckle held an edge. "It used to be that way."

They both didn't say anything for a moment. Then he broke the silence, reaching out to put a hand on her shoulder. "Those people who talked about you— they're going to be ashamed when they see that castle, when they see what you're made of."

The burn of his hand seared through her robe, flashing tendrils of warmth down her arm. She could even hear the pulse of her blood in her head, making her dizzy. "That's the idea." She laughed. "Can you imagine? Sissy Spindlebund with her 'He he he, Lacey, your last name sounds like V.D. Does that mean you have it?'"

"Everyone thought you...?" He withdrew his hand, as if the gossip could spread to him.

"Yeah, they did." She wanted to feel him again, to bask under the callused reassurance of his palm. "Not that it matters much. There were a million other reasons for me not to have a date in school."

Connor put his hand back on her. This time he traced his fingers over her biceps, using his thumb to make the inside of her arm tremble. "Don't give me stories about lacking dates. I can't believe someone like you would stay home Friday nights."

Lacey stifled a moan of longing. No one had ever touched her like this—without expectation. Deep inside, she wished Connor wasn't merely comforting her. She wished he was seducing her, riding the numbing fumes of wine that were surging through her body.

She cleared her throat, trying to get a grip. "That's sweet of you to say, Connor."

"I'm not sugar-talking you. I'm not the type."

Sugar-talking or not, she was melting inside. "How about you?" she asked. "I'll bet Connor Langley was the big man on campus, huh?"

He chuckled, his thumb lingering near the soft cove between arm and rib. Heat buzzed through her, turning her skin into sensitized bumps.

"I was a one-woman guy. Nothing fancy about that."

"A high-school sweetheart?"

He nodded. There was something so heart-wrenchingly simple about his outlook.

"And you?" he asked.

She thought about Tony, her first—and last. Thought about the discomfort of lying next to him after having lost her virginity at twenty years of age, thought about the way he'd leaned away from her when she'd told him about HazyLawn and her on-going battle with depression. She'd mistaken physical closeness for emotional connection, and she'd never repeated the error since. The rejection pained her too much.

She took a deep, cleansing breath, and Connor pulled her toward him.

Oh, God. As she relaxed in his arms, her head nestled beneath his chin, her hand resting over his mellow heartbeat, Lacey closed her eyes. She imagined for a blessed moment they could be like this forever.

She moved her fingertips over his collarbone, watching the firelight jump over his tanned skin. "I thought I had extreme feelings for another person once, but I found out I was wrong. I know better now."

"You do?"

"Yes, absolutely."

They didn't say anything for a long moment. The burning wood in the grate snapped, filling the silence's questions with a crackling response.

Maybe this was a good time to ask about his past, his home, so she slanted her head toward him. The blue moonray clarity of his waiting gaze calmed her to a sense of wordless comfort. There were no lies in the color of those eyes. Only safety, warmth.

God, now wasn't the time for talk.

Content, Lacey lay her head back on his chest and listened to the cadence of his breathing.

"Connor?"

"Yeah?"

''You're a great pillow, and you're too comfortable to let out of my house.''

His answer was to plant a hand in her hair, unfastening the bun on the back of her head, combing through the strands until she couldn't keep her eyes open from the tingly serenity of his touch.

That night, Connor slept on her couch with Lacey fitted next to him, body to body. He kept her cozy, kept her secure.

It was the first time she'd slept through the night in years.

Chapter Seven

The day was here.

Before Lacey would throw open the doors of the Spencers' old toy warehouse to reveal her castle to the multitudes, she wanted to take a second to calm down, to tell herself everything would turn out fine.

She stood before the structure, in awe of it. To think, the idea had started in her head. In fact, it had come to her way back in her HazyLawn days, when she would sit in the clinic's stone garden and fantasize. She used to think happy thoughts, like clouds and how they'd taste like cotton candy. Of grass and how every blade was its own little world. Of castles and how they were like dreams made of cut glass.

Now, it was a reality, with the high-powered lights

making the walls and turrets glimmer. She could almost imagine knights in their silver armor gleaming around the castle, guarding it, lending a sense of honor to her hopes.

The roar of an engine outside the warehouse dashed her fantasy, reminding her that people were waiting to enter.

She tore her gaze from the castle, checking to see that everything was in place: the caviar and other delicate hors d'oeuvres, the champagne and punch, the soft, atmospheric CD sound system loaded with everything from Wagner to Enya.

One more deep breath and she would be ready. She only wished Connor could be here.

Of course, she understood his reluctance to mingle with the masses. But that didn't mean she had to like it.

Lacey walked to the sliding warehouse door, then cracked it open enough so she could squeeze through and no one could catch a glimpse of the main event.

What she saw stunned her. Eight adults—her brothers and very best friends—waited with their assorted children. And that was it.

Her worst fear: having no one from town show. The lack of control tore at her, probably showing on her face.

Meg Cassidy, holding her bundled-up infant daughter Molly, flashed a warm smile. ''I'm sure more people are on their way.''

Her husband, Nick Cassidy, stepped forward to hug

Lacey. As she buried her nose in his leather jacket, she took comfort from the mild, heady scent and closed her eyes, thankful for her family and friends.

The rest of Kane's Crossing could kiss her castle for all she cared.

Nick stepped back and grabbed the hands of his two-year-old twins, Jake and Valerie. "Do we get to come in to see the eighth wonder of the world?"

The twins gave cheery little hops, squealing.

Lacey actually smiled, touched by their enthusiasm. "I suppose I could bid you enter."

A very pregnant Ashlyn Reno was the next to hug Lacey. Then she linked arms with her old friend, and Lacey noticed that Ashlyn's skin was flushed, glowing. "My hubby almost made me stay in an easy chair, but I told him I wasn't about to miss this for the world."

Lacey glanced at linebacker-shouldered Sheriff Sam Reno. "Is that right, Sam? You'd deprive me of my friend's support?"

Sam said, "She's about to give birth any minute. I'd hate to turn this place into a delivery room."

"Ooo, protective," said Ashlyn, winking at her husband. "I like that in a man."

They exchanged mysterious smiles, ones that spoke of more than flirtation. Lacey's heart clenched at the power of those looks.

She greeted Rick and his wife, Daisy, then Matt and Rachel, who also seemed ready for the birthing room at any second.

"Thanks for coming," she whispered to the lot of them.

"Are you kidding?" asked Matt, tipping back his cowboy hat so she could read his brown eyes all the better. It was clear he meant to make up for lost moments, to be the best big brother possible. "We're always here for you, Lacey."

"I know," she said. "Now, I guess it's time for you all to see what's been consuming me."

They were going to go into cardiac arrest. They were going to feel sorry for her, having spent all her savings and then some on this folly.

"Let's go then," said Rick impatiently, curling Daisy into his arms.

"Don't mind your brother," said his wife, blond curls dancing in the slight breeze. "He hasn't had his coffee today. The lack of caffeine is killing him."

"Damn straight." Rick kissed the top of Daisy's head.

"Language," said Rachel, indicating her daughter Tamela and Taggert, the Renos' son. "Little ears make great satellite dishes."

"Consider my mouth washed out with soap, Rache." Rick led Daisy toward the entrance. "Well?"

Lacey's stomach flipped. This was it.

She slid open the door, spilling the choral chants of *Carmina Burana* into the air. The triumphant music ushered the small crowd inside.

Taggert and Tamela screamed and ran toward the

castle as fast as their legs could carry them. They were dwarfed by the size of the structure, miniaturized by the walls and sparkling grandeur.

Daisy broke away from Rick. "Kids! This isn't the playground monkey bars!"

As Rick's wife caught up to the children, Rick lingered, clearly awestruck by the castle. "Whoa."

A good "whoa" or a bad "whoa"?

Lacey almost gave in to the urge to run out the door when Rick started to inspect the expensive party food. "Lace, this is…"

She didn't want to hear it. "I know."

He finally looked her in the eye. "I can't believe you pulled this off."

She wanted so badly to cling to the bright side of things: the castle's breathtaking structure, the joy on the children's faces. Yet worries flogged her. "How's the castle going to raise money for the Reno Center if it doesn't attract interest?" she asked.

Rick sent her a crooked grin. "Leave it to you to worry about the orphans."

Matt had crept up behind her, obviously overhearing the conversation. "You know damned well what's going on here."

He stepped closer, forming a circle with her and Rick. It was the first time they'd all been this close to each other, since Rick and Matt hadn't gotten along before Matt's return to Kane's Crossing.

"No, I have no idea about what's happening," she said. "All I see is that my family showed up and that's it. Not that I don't love and appreciate you all, but…''

Both of her stepbrothers glanced at the untouched mounds of hors d'oeuvres, then at each other. Then Rick spoke.

"Johann Spencer practically campaigned to keep people away from this opening. Don't you keep up with current events?''

Ire coursed through her veins. Of course. Johann. She'd seen it coming, but she'd naively thought the benefits to the Reno Center would keep him from waging this petty war.

Matt added, "There's a lot of curiosity about what you're doing. Don't worry about drawing a crowd. People will gather their courage, as they have in the past, and show up.''

"Right. I know you're right,'' she said.

Both brothers traded dark glances, probably remembering the days when she'd cried in her room and they'd done everything they could think of to get her to come out. She couldn't even remember why she'd been so sad, though she wouldn't be surprised to find out that it'd been for no reason at all.

That was depression for you. Darkness ahead, all around, swallowing you up but not bothering to digest you.

"Hey,'' she said. "Don't think I'm getting down on myself. I'm never going back to that place in my life again.''

Matt put his hand on her shoulder. "We know.''

Lacey smiled at him, thinking he probably needed the reassurance just as much as she did.

"Well, I'll be damned," said Rick.

Both Matt and Lacey followed his gaze to the entrance, where a man was sauntering toward them. Heat stole up Lacey's body, right to her face where it was no doubt marking her.

Connor.

Rachel came over and grabbed Matt's hand. "What do you know? The Kane Spencer look-alike."

"That's the rumor," said Matt. "They say he was at the last town meeting. Scared the tar out of Mrs. Spindlebund, too. She can't stop yapping about it."

"Nothing can put a halt to that woman's mouth," said Rick. "But what's he doing here?"

Lacey wanted to know the same thing.

What *was* he doing here?

Connor knew it was another bad idea to show his face in Kane's Crossing again, but he didn't much care this time.

His lawyers had determined he had a valid claim to his spot as Horatio Spencer's son, though they weren't optimistic about the man's remaining finances.

No matter. Part of Conn wanted to shout the news in the streets, while part of him wanted to remain true to his adoptive father, John Langley, and his memory.

At any rate, he was tired of hiding.

As he walked into the castle's grand opening, he couldn't contain a frown. Where were all the people?

There was Lacey, surrounded by a handful of folks he didn't know. She was watching him as if she couldn't decide how to react to his presence, as if she was confused about letting everyone know about her connection to him.

He drew up to their circle. "Just stopping by to see what all the fuss is about."

Ah, there. She'd decided how to treat him. He could tell by the invisible—but obvious—shield that had blocked her eyes. A polite, who-are-you barrier.

"Welcome," she said, nodding in greeting.

Then she turned to the rest of her crowd. "Don't mind me while I show our guest to the refreshments."

The two men—her step-brothers?—looked Conn over as if they meant to perform exploratory surgery on his intentions.

Hell, maybe Conn should do the same thing, as far as Lacey was concerned.

As she led him away, she said under her breath, "What is this about?"

"I know how much the castle means to you. I just wanted to see…"

At the refreshment table, he spied the untouched food and beverages.

She shrugged overenthusiastically. "There should be a big rush later, so I'm definitely prepared."

"Come on." Connor strained to keep from touching her, comforting her. "You can't be so flip about this. Look at how concerned your friends are. They can't stop watching you, just to see that you're okay.''

''They're looking at you, Connor. Wondering who in tarnation you are. Why did you come?''

''I wanted to be with you.'' Damn. There. He'd said it.

Lacey seemed as if she'd been blindsided by a football to the noggin. ''What?''

God. She'd heard him loud and clear. He could tell by the way she was tilting her head at him, fishing for more information, as usual.

''There was no way I could pound nails into that cabin roof while you opened up your dream for everyone to see. That's all.''

''Why, Connor. How forthcoming of you.''

''Yeah.'' The word dragged out of him, accompanied by a purposeful shake of his head.

He was getting into Lacey's life deeper and deeper.

''And speaking of being forthcoming,'' he said, ''don't tell me you're happy right now. I know the lack of response from this town has to hurt.''

A blush crept over her fragile features, suffusing her skin with so much red that her face really did resemble the shape of a heart. ''It doesn't affect me at all.''

''Bull.''

She turned on him. ''Why are you asking me these questions?''

Silence. Maybe she realized that he'd wanted to fire the same inquiry at her since they'd met. Questions that pierced the soul because he couldn't always answer them.

Lacey's friends and family watched him unwaveringly, most likely ready to pounce on him. He got the distinct impression that Lacey was their glass castle—breakable and all too clear with her heart-of-gold intentions. He wondered how far they'd go to protect her from shattering.

She sent a reassuring wave to the crowd, and they went back to their own conversations, but Conn recognized that the two men were still keeping an eye on him.

He nodded in their direction. "Your watchdogs?"

"My stepbrothers."

"I thought so."

She paused. "Are they peering at me like I've really messed up this time? Because I don't want to look too closely at their faces."

"They're concerned about you, but at the moment, I think they're more worried about the company you're keeping."

"Good." Lacey tucked a strand of dark-brown hair behind an ear. She wore it loose today so that it winged down to her shoulders. Connor couldn't tell what kind of style she was going for with the baggy sweater she'd belted around her trim waist, the long patterned skirt skimming over the curve of her hips and the heavy boots at the end of it all.

He restrained a shudder from overcoming him,

driving him into the ground with the longing to feel her skin heat under his hands.

Lacey interrupted his struggle. "I don't want them to know how disappointed I am. Is it obvious?"

"You're doing a fine job of keeping it together." And he was, too.

"It's just…" She shut her mouth, glanced at the ground.

"What?" he whispered.

She dug a boot toe into cement that had been painted to resemble lush grass strewn with flowers and rocks. "I spent so much money, took such chances. I don't know. Maybe Johann Spencer and his cronies are right. Maybe I *was* nuts to do something like this."

"Hey." He couldn't help it. He cupped her cheek with his fingers, lifting her chin until she met his gaze. Her eyes shimmered under a cover of tears. "Don't ever talk about yourself like that, Lacey Vedae. Dreams take time and a lot of disappointment. You just have to keep hoping—"

A scratching in his throat cut off the words, so he cleared it, removing his hand from Lacey's face.

She smiled up at him. "If I didn't know any better, I'd say you're trying to convince yourself of the same thing."

"I am."

As she waited for him to continue, Conn ran his gaze over her face—that innocent, gorgeous face with the large smoky blue eyes, the pointed chin, those full

lips. Somewhere along the line, someone had sprin-
kled stardust over Lacey Vedae, knowing she'd grow
into herself sooner or later.

He crossed his arms over his chest. Hell, he was in
such a protective stance you could even call his posture a coat of arms. And, all the time, he was very
aware of how Lacey's friends and family were still
staring at him.

"I've got a person in Raintree who needs me to be
in Kane's Crossing," he said, gauging her face for a
response.

Lacey's expression didn't change. In fact, Conn got
the feeling she was exerting a lot of effort to keep her
features steadied.

"This person," she asked. "Is it a woman?"

"Yeah. My mom."

She sighed, and Conn found himself hoping it was
from relief.

He continued. "Life was going along fine when,
all of a sudden, we found out that my mother,
Seonaid's her name, had non-Hodgkin's lymphoma.
Just like that. Suddenly, we were in hospitals, paying
bills we couldn't keep up with for radiation treatment.
We thought she recovered, but she relapsed and required chemotherapy. I sat by her bedside every day,
feeling like the weakest fool in creation. Powerless.
Then she told me something that changed the world."

Lacey's eyes widened, probably anticipating his
mighty twist of a secret, but he wasn't about to reveal
it. Not yet, anyway.

"I guess you could call what she told me a desperate confession," said Connor. "Even if she's in remission right now, I'm afraid she'll need more treatment, that her pain will return for good this time. There's only one way to hold back her agony, I figure. So here I am, dealing with the solution."

"Making your dreams a reality," she said, a breath of revelation in her tone.

He tried to sound more casual than he felt. "I guess so."

"I'm so sorry, Conn—"

His words whipped out. "Don't be."

Lacey's hand flew up to her face; she touched her cheek as if it'd been slapped.

Dammit. He hadn't meant to speak harshly.

A low voice broke into the awkward pause in conversation. "You doing okay, Lace?"

It was the bigger stepbrother, the one who seemed as if he could shoot a guy down with a glare.

Lacey straightened her spine, donning a sunny smile. "Yeah, Rick, I'm fine."

Conn wondered if Lacey had been pulling this act her entire life: hiding the hurt behind a different personality all together. The thought nudged at his conscience, his heart.

The crowd was drifting toward them, fringed by pregnant women, ladies holding small children and babies. When Taggert and Tamela saw Connor, they ran toward him.

"Aunt Lacey's friend," said Tamela, tugging on Conn's coat.

He greeted both young children, then tipped his hat to the rest of the assembly. They eyed him like he was a burglar who'd stumbled into the dark anticipation of a surprise party.

"Ah, yeah," said the other stepbrother. This one had a cowboy hat and denim to guard him. "Lacey's *friend.*"

Lacey merely rolled her eyes and introduced him to everyone. Afterward, she narrowed her gaze at her brothers. "Happy now?"

Rick shrugged. "To a certain degree."

A man wearing a sheriff's uniform gave Lacey a hug. "We've got to get back to the house. Ashlyn needs to be off her feet."

"Worry wart," said the woman, who'd just wandered into the group.

Conn looked once, then twice at her. Blond hair in a pixie cut, blue dominating the colors of her eyes… It was almost like peering into a warped mirror.

Ashlyn? His half sister?

As Lacey introduced them, Connor's mouth went dry. He didn't know what to say, what to do.

His sister.

Ashlyn stared at him, and everyone went silent, no doubt thinking about the Kane Spencer rumors. Then she smiled, but Conn could tell the gesture was forced, even a little stunned.

"Good to meet you...Connor?" The smile disappeared as she rubbed her distended belly.

"We need to go," said Sam, placing his palm in the small of his wife's back to lead her away. "The castle's a miracle of work, Lacey."

Time was a blur as Conn watched his sister walk out of his life. At the entrance, she paused, looked at him again, then left under the guidance of Sam Reno.

Conn barely registered the other voices as they congratulated Lacey on the castle. He was too busy remembering newspaper pictures of Horatio, and how much he was reflected in the shape of Ashlyn's jaw, the turn of her nose.

At a pause in the conversation, Conn shook himself back to reality. "I'll see Lacey home."

"I don't think—" started Matt, the cowboy brother.

"Really," said Lacey, "it's fine. Connor came to visit me anyway."

Rick started arguing with Lacey, who held her own, but Connor didn't hear much of the noise. He'd already wandered away from the stares, already ambled over to the castle.

Their voices danced among the recorded music, punctuating the lull of a violin playing a sorrowful tune.

Dreams. Castles. Cancer.

He was in over his head, and Lacey was only making life more confusing.

Chapter Eight

When everyone had cleared the warehouse, Lacey and Conn shut down the castle, dousing the lights, cleaning up the unused food, silencing the music.

At least The Wanderer would have a great upcoming meal, thought Lacey as she snapped a Tupperware lid over some salmon coated crackers garnished with cilantro and olives.

The elderly woman was due to visit her soon and, boy, was she in for a treat.

A loud click reverberated through the empty space as Connor shut off the last light. The sound caused Lacey to look up in time to see the castle shrouded by darkness. Faint brightness from the entrance loaned a bit of clarity to the room, but it still wasn't enough to keep an inner black weight from crushing Lacey's hopes for the Reno Center kids.

She heard Connor's boots thumping over the floor, then stop near her. "Ready?"

His voice held a low thunder that drove over her skin, through her body. She nodded then placed the last container in a paper bag and started hauling it away.

When they walked out of the building, Lacey tried not to look back, especially when Connor secured the rolling door. It slowly blocked the castle, inch by painful inch.

Her dream.

He sealed the door shut, locked it. Cut her off from a grand failure.

They drove back to her place in their separate vehicles, Connor cruising back into the woods to hide his truck and Lacey returning to her own home to stoke the fire and kick off her boots.

The still echo of her house invited the darkness to drag into her, numbing her into a careless void. But she wouldn't give in to it. She had family who loved her, a stranger who intrigued her. Lots to appreciate.

So instead of dwelling on the castle, she lit a Cactus Flower incense stick with flame from the fire, propped the smoking item into a holder then sank to the floor, resting her back against the couch, closing her eyes.

Too much silence. She needed noise.

She opened her eyes and turned on her wide screen

TV with the remote, flipping through the channels. Of course, nothing was on. Two hundred different satellite channels and all the programs stunk.

But the TV stayed on, almost amusing her with a cooking program on The Food Network.

"Lace?"

Connor's deep voice sent a punch of adrenaline through her. She glanced up, heart in her throat, and probably on her sleeve, too.

"Hey," she said. "You caught me daydreaming."

The fire burnished his skin, flickering soft lightning over his loose hair. He resembled a hard-edged angel who'd gotten lost during a naughty joyride out of Heaven.

"I apologize for walking on into your home," he said. "I knocked at the kitchen door, but you didn't answer."

She'd almost missed the chance to be with him again, all because she'd tuned out.

Maybe today she was much closer to being that weighted-down, sensitive teenager than she realized. Maybe her friends and family saw the shadow of her past inching over her when she'd failed to notice it herself.

Lacey took care to spread out her skirt in apparent carelessness, tucking it under her legs. Then she patted the floor next to her. "Take a load off."

He slid to the carpet, so close that the rough material of his homespun shirt scratched against Lacey's sweater. She could feel the bulk of his biceps rubbing against her own arm, reminding her of his physical strength, the force of his presence.

"Damn," he said, shaking his head as he watched her.

He drew up his legs and leaned his forearms against his lower thighs. "You still look as pitiful as a puppy in a pet store cage."

"I'm glad to know that I come off with such a degree of sophistication. A puppy?"

"Puppies are cute."

Lacey smiled, then stared at the fire more intently. "You know, women don't take too kindly to being called that."

"You made that clear the first night we met. Remember?"

She turned back to him. "I—"

He was grinning. The devil-may-care guy was actually taking a measure of amusement from this whole conversation.

"What's so funny?" she asked.

He was so near she couldn't help noticing the cut-glass sparkle in his blue eyes. "I like your feistiness."

So he was being a good guy, trying to cheer her up. The sweet hunk.

The seed of a laugh bloomed in the back of her throat, starting out as a giggle. Then it grew, branching out. The laughter cleansed her. "How is it that you bring out the best in me?" she asked.

His fingers worked their way to the back of her neck, where they massaged the knot there.

"I've got nothing to do with it. You're naturally a good person."

She took a deep breath, a shudder waving through her body as his fingers spread from her neck to inside the collar of her sweater, where they rubbed over her bare shoulder.

Pull yourself together, she told herself. And she did, battling the urge to fall into him, to give herself to this man, heart and soul. But the soul part would mean exposing her secrets to him, and she wouldn't chance that. Not if she wanted him to keep looking at her with that admirable light in his eyes.

He used his other hand to tenderly smooth a strand of hair away from her face. His touch lingered on her cheek, the pads of his fingers strumming the hollow of bone, the slant of her chin.

Lacey's eyelids shut involuntarily, but she forced them back open, afraid to give in to the heat that was causing an electrical storm to zap through her lower stomach.

During the pause in their words, the TV became much too loud, as if it were attempting to bring her back to her senses. Connor must've been aware of the useless noise, too, because he liberated the remote from its spot on the floor and muted the volume, tossing the device on the couch.

"Come here," he said, shifting his body in order to cuddle her back against his chest.

His long legs barred her on both sides, and she rested her arms on them, finally relaxing under the toastiness of the fire, the scent of Cactus Flower incense, the feel of his hand in her hair. His other arm crossed her chest, his palm resting on her shoulder as she leaned her cheek against the back of his hand.

He played with her hair, and the sensation sent lazy swirls of longing through her. "You're going to put me to sleep."

When he laughed, she moved with him, the vibrations from his broad chest echoing over her skin. "Has anyone ever told you that you've got the softest hair?"

"It's what they call 'fine.' Doesn't hold its curl." She could feel him twirl a lock around his finger, her head moving with his gentle effort.

"I don't much care for ringlets. Besides, you've outgrown girlish vanities."

"I thought you said I was cute."

She could feel him unwinding his finger from her hair. Then, with slow strokes, he toyed with the strands above her ear.

Whoa. A few more minutes of this and he'd be able to talk her into anything. He'd reduce her body to putty with the way he was handling her.

"You did come off as a little snow bunny that first day I met you," he said. "Nose wiggling, ears standing straight up, soft as dandelion down…"

"Boy." She thought back to that day. Okay. So the perky gloves and earmuffs hadn't been the best clothes choice she'd ever made. No wonder he'd called her "cute."

"But you've got a core of steel," he said. "And you're definitely all woman."

Awareness roared from the tips of her toes to the lobes of her ears. It throbbed on every nerve ending.

All woman?

Even today, when she'd been getting ready to go to the castle opening, she hadn't seen an adult female staring back in the mirror at her. She'd seen Lacey Vedae, same as she always was, struggling to find herself in every hidden corner of life.

She needed to say something light here, something that would keep her from turning right around and planting a kiss on his mouth. The last thing she could afford was to chase Connor away with an overzealous attempt at affection.

"All woman," she said, laughing a little. "Not even a bit goddess?"

His fingers traced over her scalp with the tempo of a wicked lullaby. "I didn't want you to get arrogant."

How could she not, with this sort of attention? She felt like the most beautiful girl in the world with his hands caressing her.

He tilted her face toward him, and Lacey caught her breath. While she'd been faced away from him, he'd gotten all worked up, judging from the flames reflected in his eyes.

"Somehow," he said, "I think you have no idea how much you test me."

Test *him?* Her? She was just an average woman with more-than-average concerns.

She looked toward the fire again, pulse raging with the possibility of what he was insinuating. "Conn, be serious."

He exhaled, then settled his arm over her chest once more, his palm on her shoulder. She leaned against the back of his hand again, feeling his veins against her cheek.

He chuffed, his voice low. "I am serious, Lace. Dammit, more than you know."

Was that her heartbeat filling the room? Or maybe it was his, echoing through his chest and into her ear.

What if this was a repeat of Tony? They'd make love. They'd talk in the afterglow and, in her loose-limbed happiness, she'd tell him all about the therapists, her secret shames. Then he'd leave, just like Tony.

Maybe she should skip to the part where she told him and he disappeared. Maybe with her back to his chest, she could avoid the shock of his gaping mouth, the blankness of his eyes, when she told him the news.

Could she preempt the hurt? Test the waters by revealing her background little by little?

As she spoke, her lips moved against his hand. She could feel his breathing quicken in his chest.

"There's something I want to tell you about…" Wait. She wouldn't let him know about HazyLawn. Not now. "I had…have issues. Nothing more than most people."

His hand—the one that had been stroking her

hair—moved down to her throat, his fingers sketching over the pulse of it, the sensitive center, tickling her with shivers.

"What kind of issues?" he asked.

"Well…" *Tell him. Get it over with. See if he'll run now or later.* "…I was a real depressed kid. You would've cringed at the sight of me."

"Don't say that." His voice was so soft, so gentle, that she wanted to collapse with relief.

But it was too early for that.

"No, really. I alienated half my friends, made my family incredibly nervous. But I couldn't control my sadness, my anxiety. Even something as silly as a boy in junior high walking past me without smiling would turn my day into a living hell."

"So you weren't just a normal, withdrawn teen? It was really serious?"

Lacey nodded against his hand, loving the coarse feel of his skin against her cheek. He turned his palm upward to cup her face, and she stayed that way, closing her eyes as she continued.

"A lot of people think depression is something that everyone goes through. That it's easy to pull out of. All you have to do is not feel sorry for yourself. But it's not like that at all. It steals your energy, makes you a zombie. And, most times, you *do* care. You want to please your mother…or other people…so badly that it kills you when you fail."

She took a breath, wondering if she'd lost him yet. Usually, at this point, most folks would dismiss her story as that of a spoiled girl, a girl who had everything except tragedy, so she'd created some for herself by lapsing into this attention-grubbing malady.

Heck, he was still holding her, caressing her, so maybe he hadn't turned on her yet.

She ventured more explanation. "I guess grade school was the first time I remember feeling so badly that it ached. My mom and I had gotten in a huge fight about how I dressed. This is when our war started: I'd try to push her buttons with the most outrageous outfits possible. Then I realized I got a reaction from everyone else, too. I liked it. I was able to control what they thought of me. Unfortunately, my mom considered this a rebellion, and it caused a rift between us."

"Your stepbrothers. Didn't they help you?" Connor asked.

"Sure. They stood up for me all the time. But nothing could help me and Mom. I was already too angry with her for moving from marriage to marriage. The wedding to Russell Shane was number three, you know. And my real dad... He's out of the picture. Ditched us when I was still in diapers."

"That's unforgivable."

Connor bent down to press a soft kiss on her temple, causing Lacey to tremble deep in her stomach.

Uncontrollable stirrings of an awakening hunger.

He adjusted their position so she was nearer to him, so close his breath warmed her ear.

"That's how it is, Connor. I blamed Mom for everything. It's funny, though. I cared a lot about her. Cared too much about many things. Then I started not to care. My grades gradually hit rock bottom in junior high school. I started dressing in black just to tick off my mom even more—not that it mattered so much. I was lonely, numb and bored. There were nights I couldn't sleep, even though my eyes burned from crying.''

She paused, knowing the story would have to end here if she didn't want to talk about checking into HazyLawn her freshman year of high school or the couple of relapses she'd had since then.

Connor had started slowly rocking her back and forth, as if she needed to be coaxed into the sleep she'd missed during her childhood. ''I can't imagine you as that girl.''

Some days, she couldn't fathom it, either. But it was true. She'd suffered a severe depression that had marked her as cleanly as…

No. She wasn't going to think about that. Was *never* going to talk about that.

''Don't worry,'' she said. ''I'm over it.''

She glanced back at him and smiled. But, somehow, it didn't feel real.

She had all her hopes in her gaze, and the sight nearly slayed him.

Connor couldn't picture a Lacey whose smile didn't work quite right. One who'd probably hung her head and allowed her soft hair to hide her face so she wouldn't have to talk to anyone. One who'd dressed like a member of a funeral party.

Funeral.

He banished the thought, the hovering reminder of his mom's tenuous health. He'd never allow her to die when he could prevent it.

Never.

Lacey's smile—what there was of it—wilted, and he realized that he'd been holding her a little too tightly, too possessively.

Relaxing his embrace, Conn leaned his head into her neck, craving her sweet tangerine scent. She snuggled against him, pressing the back of his head as if asking for more.

Damn, that flash of desire was back again, needling him, filling him with a fierce urge to be surrounded by her heat.

Without a thought to consequence, he shifted, found himself crushing his lips against hers with as much passion as he'd felt that night under Kane Spencer's statue. Then, the snow had slivered against their faces with icy kisses. Now, the fire spurred him with its own shards of lust, jabbing him on with a combination of wanting to soothe Lacey and just plain wanting her.

He sipped at her lips, tasting traces of the air's exotic incense, pulling at her bottom lip with an urgency that goaded him to ignore every gentlemanly cell in his body.

Wait. He couldn't expect Lacey to be his balm.

Couldn't expect something so emotionally demanding from a woman this fragile and in need of comfort.

Slow down.

He tried. He really did. But when he slowed down, she sped up, testing his mouth with her tongue, savoring his lips, delving into him with an innocent insistence that banished every chivalrous thought he owned.

She pushed him back into the couch, turning herself around so that she straddled him, her skirt spreading over his legs to envelop them both. She leaned forward, her hands cupping his jawline, her kisses heating every inch of his skin as he held up his hands in weak surrender.

Was he really going to do this? Take advantage of Lacey's bad day merely to give in to his sexual drive? He wanted her so badly that this situation was tempting.

He felt her working at the buttons on his shirt, and that was that. He couldn't fight her *and* himself.

When her fingers tangled in her haste, he helped her by unbuttoning the remaining wooden discs, then parting the material so that the air hit his bare chest. Then, damn, she traced her hands up and down his skin, her fingers grooving into his ribs, her palms glancing over his nipples, hardening them into sensitive nubs. Desire roared through his lower belly, gathering in the bulge of his arousal.

He sank lower against the couch, bent his legs slightly so that Lacey glided against the hardness be-

tween his legs, so that she could feel the consequences of her innocuous kisses.

She gasped, and he hesitated, giving her the opportunity to rethink what she was doing.

No chance of that. As she leaned over to lay her
hands on his chest once again, she wiggled against
him, making him groan.

She'd asked for it.

Conn slipped under her sweater, one hand on the
small of her back to further urge her against him, one
hand traveling up her toned stomach, her rib cage, to
fill itself with a small, shapely breast. He rubbed a
thumb over the crest of it, feeling it harden, heat up
under the silk of her bra.

As they moved together, locked into a rocking
rhythm, Conn found her mouth again, ravished it with
more kisses.

He hadn't ever felt this kind of burning lust, this
need to push against her—into her—without a care to
the ramifications.

He dragged his lips from Lacey's mouth to her
neck, to the spot beneath an ear, tonguing it, nipping
at her lobe.

It'd never been like this with another woman before.

But was this the right thing to be doing with Lacey?
A woman who'd just told him about her delicate mental past?

"Lacey," he said, dragging himself away from her
kisses.

She stopped, frozen, her gaze uncertain. Then she peered down, at his hand on her breast. "I…oh."

As she began to slip away from him, he held on to her. "Wait. Don't go anywhere."

"But you…?"

What the hell was he doing?

He was having a conscience, that's what. By God, he hated manners.

"Lace, I'm not sure this is the best moment to be with you."

Toughest words he'd ever muttered.

This time she succeeded in climbing off him, in breaking the raging-blood contact of his hands on her skin and her weight against his. She stood and straightened her sweater, her skirt, her hair.

"You're not taking advantage of anything. I have a brain, you know. I'm pretty good at making decisions."

Conn started buttoning his shirt, unsure of what else to do. She seemed damned angry. And why? Because he was being nice.

Well, damn nice.

"You just got finished telling me about your sorrows and I lost it. I'm sorry."

"Don't you dare apologize." She fisted her hands on her hips, gaze blazing him. "Listen, Connor Langley. After my *delicate condition* improved, my family and friends handled me with kid gloves, as if I'd crumble if they treated me like a normal human being. Well, they've gotten over that, partly because I didn't react too well to being coddled like a cracked china doll who needs mending. I won't stand for you tiptoeing around me, either. Jeez, I was afraid this would happen.''

This is what he got for considering her situation?

All he could do was stand, nod to her in silent farewell then shake his head in disbelief. If he would've dared say anything to her, she would've bitten off his head, so he best not say a damned word.

As he left, Lacey had one more comment.

''I'm not that glass castle, Connor. Don't treat me like one.''

Her words rang in his ears as he walked away, scraped and jagged as the edges of a broken hope.

Chapter Nine

Years ago, Chaney's Drugstore had been decimated, the victim of a bomb Chad Spencer had set off. But the business had risen from the ashes with the help of Nick Cassidy, just as Lacey had done. Yet, in spite of everything she'd accomplished, doubts always lingered, waiting to flare up and reduce her to nothing again.

Days later, as she sat in a booth at the new Chaney's Drugstore with Ashlyn Spencer Reno, Lacey still couldn't get Connor—and their steamy encounter—off her mind.

Had she really been so forward with him? Had that been her, Lacey Vedae, hopping onto his lap and tearing open his shirt while smothering him with kisses?

Her body warmed up just thinking about it.

"Earth to Lacey," said Ashlyn, staring at her friend over the glass rim of a low-fat natural strawberry fruit shake. "Is there anything behind that vacant stare?"

Lacey was tempted to tell Ashlyn all about Connor: about how he left silly gifts such as pinecone men and pine-needle bouquets at her doorstep in the days since their wonderful, yet doomed, make-out session. About how he'd gone back to playing mystery man in the cabin, though his thoughtful presents told Lacey he hadn't rejected her entirely.

Yup. After her initial anger at the way he'd halted their lovemaking, she'd realized that maybe he'd only been scared away by her aggressive jump-his-bones curiosity, not by stories of her depression. But, hey, it'd been so long since a man had touched her she hadn't been able to help herself.

She smiled, replaying the night. He hadn't turned tail and ran when she'd told him about her past. Finally, someone who could accept all of Lacey—problems and everything.

Maybe he was even the man who wouldn't be shocked by her stay in HazyLawn.

Across the table, Ashlyn inspected Lacey's absent giddiness, giving her the visual third degree. Narrowing her eyes, Ashlyn probably expected her to 'fess up about whatever was consuming her thoughts.

Isn't that what women did on these sorts of outings—complained about men? Lacey wasn't sure, since she'd never really dated much and, thus, didn't have many male problems.

"I'm just spacing out," she said, deciding to keep Connor to herself.

Sigh. *All* to herself.

Ashlyn settled back into the vinyl puffiness of the booth's seat, her stomach pooched like a world-champion Bazooka gum bubble. Lively country music twanged through the establishment, encouraging the mostly teenaged patrons to desert their stools at the counter and dance on the parquet floor. The smell of chocolate ice cream and maraschino cherries hovered over the eating area and shopping aisles, making Chaney's rebuilt drugstore a popular hangout in Kane's Crossing.

Ashlyn said, "Don't tell me I asked you here for nothing. Sam and Taggert are likely to give me grief when they find out I disobeyed the doc's orders to take it easy during the day. I tell you, my feet swell up like water balloons, and yet I left my recliner to watch you moon over your chocolate malt?"

"Hey, I can't stop you from ignoring advice. I tend to agree with Sam. We both care about your comfort."

"You're a bunch of worry warts." Ashlyn waved a dismissive hand at Lacey. "I've never felt better in my life. Who says pregnancy is tough?"

A gaggle of Kane's Crossing's finest gossips ambled into the ice-cream shop area. As they settled themselves at the counter, ordering from the white-aproned soda jerk, they cast glances at Lacey and Ashlyn.

"Here we go," said Ashlyn, unruffled as an ironed spring skirt. Yet she rubbed her belly as if to calm her expected child. "Ever since Johann took possession of my old stomping grounds, the taunts have increased tenfold."

Lacey wondered how Ashlyn stood for the gossip, her being a black-sheep Spencer and all. "It's not as if you miss the mansion. So why does what they say matter?"

"It doesn't. They don't seem to realize that losing my home, my fortune and my family wasn't as bad as it sounds. I'd choose Sam and Taggert over my old life any day of the week."

Her family had ostracized her because she'd unearthed evidence of their past crimes. Once again, Lacey couldn't help wondering what Ashlyn would do if Connor turned out to be another Spencer. If he ended up being another blood relative who had the potential to disappoint her.

Ashlyn stared out the window, where Johann Spencer and his cronies descended upon the shop. Lacey kept her cool, averting her eyes from the unwelcome sight.

"Who was that man at the castle opening?" asked Ashlyn.

"I can't believe you didn't ask me sooner."

"I feel silly even talking about this, but…"

"Ashlyn, you know I'd do about anything for you,

but I already made a promise to Connor that I wouldn't talk about him.'' Lacey sighed. ''I'd give my right arm to be able to tell you more…''

''But you're as good as your word.'' Ashlyn smiled, placed one of her hands over Lacey's. ''I know. It's one of the reasons I value your friendship. Everyone is gossiping about the stranger who looks like Kane Spencer, and I just need to know what's going on. It's driving Johann crazy. I'd love to add to his confusion.''

''Here, here.'' Lacey held up her malt in a salute, which Ashlyn imitated.

As they both sipped from their straws, Johann Spencer glided into the shop, flanked by several dark-coated men in black glasses. He took a seat near the other Spencer supporters. His employees, fans…whatever they were…stayed standing. Then he ordered ''the usual.''

''Doesn't this just make your day, too?'' asked Ashlyn.

''I'd like a word with that arrogant fool,'' said Lacey, watching Johann. ''He's keeping people from the castle.''

''You mean, he's convinced most of Kane's Crossing to stay away from it. Sam told me that more and more tourists are visiting. Word-of-mouth is spreading. It's going to flourish, Lacey, don't worry.'' Ashlyn speared a glare in Johann's direction.

He was already peering at them. As the soda jerk placed ice-cream sundaes in front of the Spencer menagerie, Johann mumbled something to the man. The employee skittered over to the stereo system to turn down the volume.

"I seem to be in the right place at the right time," he said in his Euro-accent. "Good afternoon, Ms. Vedae. Mrs. Reno."

He tossed off Ashlyn's name as if it wasn't good enough to weigh on his tongue for more than a millisecond. Ashlyn merely sent him a mocking smile. Lacey nodded to him and turned back to her friend, hoping Johann would practice some courtesy and leave them to their drinks.

Like that was going to happen.

"You ladies do not wish to speak with me?" he asked. "Pity. At least when I come in here during the week, Deacon Chaney has the grace to tell me outright that he cannot tolerate my company. I like his spirit."

"Johann," said Ashlyn, her saccharine smile turned to utter contempt, "we're trying to be polite. Would you grant the favor of ignoring us?"

Lacey almost laughed at Ashlyn's pseudoetiquette, the way she was clipping her words and holding her head.

"Ashlyn, how can I possibly turn away from the two people who give me the most grief in this town?"

Lacey muttered to Ashlyn. "Here we go with the castle land again."

"Ms. Vedae…" began Johann.

"What did I tell you?" she whispered.

Ashlyn shrugged, diving back into her health shake, concerning herself with more important matters.

Johann continued. "I hear your castle endeavor is close to being a failure. Is that true?"

His cronies laughed. But Lacey couldn't help noticing that other people in the ice-cream shop, namely the teens who'd been dancing to the stifled music, didn't react. Maybe she had some allies here.

Years of turned-up noses, muttered gossip and Kane's Crossing backstabbing goaded her. Johann couldn't jump on top of the established dog pile without her trying to knock him off. "You can't keep the tourists away from something they want to see," she said, glaring at him. "Not unless you set up roadblocks."

"I will consider it," he said, much to the amusement of his company. "The lack of public response to your inane attempt to steal my land must be humiliating for you. *Depressing.* One has to wonder about your condition, your judgment when it comes to building wasteful monuments and keeping company with strange men who creep into town meetings and simply disappear."

Ashlyn's head shot up from her drink.

Johann added, "That impaired behavior should put you back in…what do they call them here in America?"

"Loony bins," said one of his people.

"Ah, yes. Loony bins. I shudder to think of life in a place like that."

Red veiled her vision. Red like anger. Red like mortification.

As she spoke, her voice held a slice of retribution. "I think life in the Spencer mansion isn't too far from loony, Johann. If you'd like to speak to me in private, feel free. Otherwise, I'm sure Ashlyn's husband—*the sheriff*—would be more than happy to escort you back to your... What do they call it here in America? Oh, yes. Den of Iniquity."

Johann didn't say anything for a moment. Then he burst out laughing, and his contingency followed suit. Pretty soon they were all paying more attention to their sundaes than Ashlyn and Lacey.

Spent, Lacey couldn't breathe, couldn't function under the image of HazyLawn, the reminder that no one in Kane's Crossing had forgotten. Would never forget.

"I've got work to do," she said to Ashlyn, while grabbing her purse.

"They're clowns, Lacey. Finish your malt."

"No, really. I've got more of a life than Johann Spencer does, so I've got to go."

Ashlyn's rainbow-colored eyes went soft. "I'm going to have a chat with Johann. This is as good an opportunity as any."

Lacey realized she was shaking, having danced too close to the town's opinion of her. Rage was swelling in her chest, threatening to drown her. She wanted to leave on a gust of class, staying a level above Johann.

"Don't stay too long, Ashlyn. Be careful."

"You know I'll be okay," said her friend. "Johann talks a good game, but he has nothing over me."

Lacey nodded, unable to speak. The ice-cream shop was closing in on her, smothering her with that mottled red lack of control.

Go home.

Get out before they see you break into a million furious pieces.

She rushed out of the shop, pushed along by the high-pitched, sarcastic calls of "bye-bye" from her enemies at the counter. But at least she'd retained her dignity.

When she got into her car, she tried to stop her trembling, her stomach-churning loss of composure.

Jerking the cell phone from her purse, Lacey dialed Dr. Franco's office, praying he had time to listen. Time to hear about everything: the gossip, the castle.

And how she feared Conn, like most of Kane's Crossing, wouldn't accept her for who she was. Flaws and all.

Connor heard Lacey pull up her driveway from his perch on the roof where he was making the last of the repairs. Even though he'd done his best to stay out of her way since the other night—except for those silly little woodland gifts he'd been leaving at her doorstep, just for the hell of it, and maybe to quell her disappointment in him, too—he still couldn't erase the need to see her perky smile, her sparkling eyes.

But he didn't do anything about it, even though his binoculars rested right next to him, waiting, mocking him with the possibility of catching a glimpse of Lacey again.

The sound of a closing door echoed through the air, and Connor stopped his work.

After fighting his better judgment for about fifteen minutes, he raised those damned binoculars to his gaze, merely to see if Lacey had come outside. Merely to check on her. Right?

Right.

And there she was, jamming his breath down his throat, just by appearing. She sat on a bench in her Japanese stone garden, sun reflecting off the snow-patched ground to shine upon her upturned face, her dark hair. As she leaned back, supported by her arms, Connor imagined running his hands over her smooth skin, the slight curves of her body.

He lowered the binoculars. What had he become? One of those drooling losers he'd read about in big city papers, guys who spied from their apartment windows on lonely ladies?

Hell. This was ridiculous, staying out here in the woods. Maybe enough time had passed since that night, enough time to allow the return of that comfort he'd experienced with her, talking in easy tones, holding each other against the night's chill.

Okay, maybe not holding each other. That's what had started this cold war between them.

He glanced toward Lacey again, seeing that she was still basking in the soft sunlight. It was time to face her, to get past this foolishness.

He took his time coming down from the roof. The fact that his real father had died from a fall never escaped Connor's attention; it haunted him, reminded him of his duty to remain true to the good man who'd raised him.

As he walked past the cover of trees, he told himself that renewing their acquaintance was a fine idea, a necessity if he wanted to stay in Lacey's good graces.

But he didn't expect the slow implosion that swelled through him as he stood in front of her.

As he weakened, second by second, just by watching her, she seemed to ignore him, breathing deeply, in…out…in…

Finally, she opened her eyes, her head resting against a shoulder as she sent a demure glance his way. Is this what she'd look like with her head on a pillow, veiled with the heat he'd bring to her face with the play of his fingers and hands?

"Thought I'd take in some air," she said, grinning at him. "Sometimes breathing can change your whole attitude. Did you know that?"

Her smile was so genuine that he lit up, too, returning the gesture while shaking his head. Funny how Lacey Vedae, someone unconnected to him by blood or history, could be so happy to see him. Could accept him without explanation, unconditionally, without making him want to change one speck of his identity.

"Why do you need an alteration of attitude?"

She paused, and he noticed she took another long breath, another endless exhalation.

Something was off-kilter. Even in such a short time, he'd gotten to know enough about her to discern a bad Lacey moment. Unable to help himself, Connor sank to the stone bench beside her, offering support, if not much more.

"What is it?" he asked.

She wilted a little, lowering her gaze from his. "Everything's come to a head, I think. And I'm not sure I'm handling it very well."

Her voice wobbled a bit, and Connor instinctively brushed her shoulder with his hand. "What do you mean?"

"All the gossip. Johann. The castle." Another pause. "Other matters."

This time, Conn didn't hold back. He hated to see Lacey's eyes go wide and sad. He took her chin between two fingers, turned her face toward him.

"Tell me," he said.

She sighed against his touch, melting the area behind his rib cage with something deeper than lust, than memories of the other night. She spilled the afternoon's events to him: the castle speculation, the rumors about her "keeping company" with the Kane Spencer lookalike, the taunting about her depression.

Conn's protective temper flared.

"Why do you allow them to matter?" he asked, jaw clenched. At the same time, he wondered the same thing about his own life.

Why *did* the Spencers matter so damned much?

"Because…" She closed her eyes. "I try to tell myself that they're nothing. That they don't have the power to affect me. But, you know what? They do. Because they know things that I haven't…" She seemed to choke on her words.

"What?"

Then, with that inner strength Conn admired, she regrouped. "They know things I haven't told you yet."

She sat forward, blocking him out with her posture.

"You don't have to say anything if you don't want to."

"If I could, I'd keep it a secret forever. But the town knows, and I figure I should tell you before they do." She shook her head. "Even my doctor agrees. I need to spill the beans."

She shot him a gauging look, but a jolt of panic caused Connor's eyebrow to lift before he could contain his shock.

"Doctor?" he asked softly. "Are you okay?"

She laughed slightly, an undercurrent of trouble lining the sound. "It's not the type of doctor you're thinking of. He's a therapist. *My* therapist. I go once a week.''

Maybe she expected him to jump out of his seat and blaze a trail of fire as he ran away from her. Her expression told him she wouldn't have been surprised.

''Go on,'' he said, resting his hand on her shoulder, his fingers cupping her ear, stroking her, calming her.

She bit her lip, mouth twitching downward as it fought a frown. After another moment of silence, she continued. ''I told you about my depression. The town got such a kick out of it. Just another item on the gossip agenda, right? But it got so bad my freshman year of high school that I…''

He waited, half hoping he wouldn't have to put her through the pain of remembering.

But she went on. ''…I started cutting myself with a razor blade.''

''You tried to commit suicide?''

''No, no.'' She shook her head, as if attempting to figure it out herself. ''I didn't know what I was doing. I lightly cut my palm, just to see if I could control the pain. Just to see if my mom would notice. I can't really explain it, not even today, but the doctors speculated I was acting out.''

Thank God. She hadn't been ending her life. But he still couldn't comprehend this.

She said, ''Rick noticed the wounds. Of course, he went crazy, told my parents. We agreed to check in to a place in Louisville called HazyLawn, a clinic where I'd receive the attention of therapists. A place that would give me peace and time to reflect. There, I went through therapy and took Prozac. Eventually, I did get better. The medication really helped.''

"Do you still take it?''

"Yes, every morning.'' She was watching him closely again. "I've been on it for the past six months, ever since I relapsed. It was right before Matt came home, and I was worried about his wife Rachel....''

Frustration prodded him to say, "You worry too much about others.'' But isn't that what drew him to her? Her openness, her nurturing spirit?

"I'd do anything for the people I love.'' Her glance rested on him a beat too long, but she tore away her gaze before he could react.

Was she hinting...?

She straightened her spine, all business, all avoidance. "I had another episode before the one I just mentioned, though, right after the end of a bad relationship.'' She smiled, picked at her skirt. "I guess I'm doomed to a life of therapy, huh?''

"Why the hell do you stay in Kane's Crossing, Lacey? God.'' Anger raced through Conn again. "Are you telling me there're people in this town who taunt you about your mental illness?''

She didn't answer the question. "You can go now, if you want. I don't expect you to sit here and make me feel better.''

His hand tightened on her shoulder. "Is that what *you* want?''

"No." She pressed her lips together, swallowed, then repeated, "No."

"Good. Because, frankly, I'm rooted to the spot." He shot her a bolstering grin.

She stared at him a moment, as if hardly believing that he wasn't giving her a tougher time about her confession. "You don't care?"

"Yeah, I care. About you." And he did—way too much.

Her answering laugh came out on a disbelieving hitch, followed by a whispered, "Thank God," as she nestled against his chest, the breath easing out of her, shoulders relaxing as if she'd shirked off the world's weight. Conn held Lacey against him, surrounding her with his arms, blocking everything else out.

So much for no more holding each other. Not that he minded.

"I was so afraid to talk you about the extent of my problems," she said.

"Why? It's not like I'm perfect."

She didn't say anything in response to his comment. "I just rehashed everything with Dr. Franco today. You know, it's so hard to tell the truth about who you are. There's the possibility that the whole story will chase people away. But I had to do it, especially since the town is buzzing about my past again, thanks to Johann."

The truth about who you are.

Connor's grip on Lacey tightened. He wanted to

tell her all about himself, too, but he couldn't. Not now.

Not when he was a member of the last family she wanted to have in her backyard.

He swerved the subject back to her. "So you thought I was going to hate you for the truth?"

"I know. Ridiculous, isn't it?" Now that she'd come clean, Lacey's words flowed with more confidence. "It's that same stubbornness that brought me back to Kane's Crossing after I got out of HazyLawn. I'd gone through a high school program there. I graduated. My stepdad wanted me to help with Shane Industries, and I wanted to be with him. Even if Rick and Matt had gone their own ways, even if my mom had split for Vegas by then, I still wanted my dad. He gave me purpose in life, encouraged me, told me I was going to be a success."

"You are a success." He laid his cheek against the top of her head, closing his eyes, wishing he were half the person she was. "You're a sight better than any one of these people in town."

She sat up, facing him. She felt so relaxed, so happy now. And why not? She'd gotten a load off her chest. "You know what I should do?"

"What?"

"I should go right back to Chaney's Drugstore and give Johann a piece of my mind. I shouldn't have allowed him to make me so angry that I had to leave." She widened her eyes, her spiky lashes like thorns. "He's never going to get the best of me again."

"That's something I'd like to see. Johann Spencer put in his place."

"Then come with me."

Right.

He chuckled, words rushing out of him before he could think twice. "You, my lady, are pure gold."

Pure gold. What did that mean? Did it have something to do with love?

Hell no. He admired Lacey, respected her above all others in Kane's Crossing. She'd proven her loyalty by keeping his presence a secret, by housing him and feeding him with the greatest of care.

He didn't have time for love, so he'd best not mix up his emotions. Honoring her and loving her were two different things.

Still, he'd give anything to see Johann squirm, especially since he had the low-down guts to be teasing Lacey about her castle, tormenting her about her past.

Hell, he'd even like to get in a few good cuffs at the man, as well. The more he thought about how Johann treated Lacey, the more necessary comeuppance seemed.

"Let's go for a drive," he said, standing and holding his hand out so Lacey could grab on to it.

Their gazes connected, bonded by her forthcoming nature and his will to see justice done. But when she laid her palm in his, trusting him, her touch divided his own loyalties.

Splitting his conscience right down the middle.

* * *

Lacey had hopped into her car and driven with Connor to the drugstore, ready to rumble.

Did she intend to bite as fiercely as she'd barked? Or did the rush of knowing that Connor accepted her, psychological warts and all, make her braver than she really was?

God, she'd been scared witless as she'd told him about Dr. Franco, the Prozac, the cutting. But he'd absorbed her truths with stoic reassurance.

No wonder she'd fallen for him.

As they pulled into a parking space, she stopped fidgeting, reeling from the thought. Love. Was she setting herself up for a disappointment? It was one thing to have Connor accept all her faults as a friend, but could he ever return her feelings, knowing about all her imperfections?

She glanced at him as he waited behind the driver's wheel. Now that they were shielded among the townspeople's trucks and Johann's contingent of town cars and utility vehicles, Connor had changed. It was almost as if he sensed Johann's presence in the metal, the chrome and lacquered paint jobs. He was locked into the guise of a man she'd never want to cross in a million years. An avenging, falling being from the skies, sword points gleaming in the blue of his eyes, his pale hair loose around his shoulders.

"Here we are," he said. Even his voice had lowered to a rumble, a roll of storm warning and tension.

She pulled her coat around her. "Maybe you should stay out here."

"And miss this?" His brow slashed above one eye, the line of it raised and aimed. "I'll be there, Lacey, even if I'm in the shadows, just watching."

And waiting. The picture of him blending with darkness gave her a dangerous thrill because, really, she didn't know Connor Langley. Hadn't heard his entire story, his reason for being in Kane's Crossing.

Though she did have her suspicions.

"Let's go," he said, opening the driver's door.

She felt a little dizzy, a little too full of his power. But she got out of the car, walking side by side with Connor as his coat caught the air and flapped into her, beating against her hip with the cadence of a war song.

They cut through the aisles, following the restored country music to the ice-cream counter. As chocolate syrup sweetness invaded her senses, she saw that a new group of teens were dancing, but Johann's crew was still at the counter, sipping on malts now. Johann, himself, was ensconced in Ashlyn's booth, where she was wagging her finger at him.

Great. Ashlyn had to be stubborn, refusing to go back home for some much needed rest. Why couldn't she listen to doctor's orders?

As Johann caught sight of Lacey, her stomach clenched, steadying itself. She didn't even check to see if Connor had ducked into an adjoining aisle. Just feeling his presence as enough to steel her.

"Johann," she said, nodding.

"Ms. Vedae." He didn't even bother to get out of his seat. "Good. My far-removed cousin here was growing tiresome."

Ashlyn turned a surprised glance on Lacey, then she smiled, clearly relieved that her friend had returned. "Run while you have the chance," she said, winking, conveying she'd held her own in the conversation with Johann.

"Yes," he said, "run. And take the castle with you."

"Funny you should bring that up," said Lacey, stepping forward. "It's time we talked, Johann, and—"

The man opened his mouth to add his own two-million cents.

She cut him off, lifting up an index finger. "—Don't interrupt me."

His mouth stayed open, and Lacey's lungs swelled with satisfaction. She exhaled, unable to stop a grin from covering her mouth.

Odd. Johann's jaw was still unhinged, and Ashlyn's eyes looked ready to pop out of her head....

Connor's heavy footsteps knocked some sense into her. The thumps echoed off the walls, coming to rest just behind Lacey.

By now, the whole room was statue-blank. Mouths agape. Limbs frozen.

The mysterious stranger, right here in the drugstore.

Ashlyn's eyes hadn't returned to normal size, but

they were overshadowed by Johann's shape as he emerged from the booth, feet apart, jaw tensed. The music lowered once again.

"You," he said.

"I hear you've been giving my friend some grief," said Connor. "I hear you've said some damned awful things."

Damn, Connor. He hadn't planned to stay in the shadows, and Lacey felt like a fool for not realizing it. He'd wanted a piece of Johann Spencer, and she'd provided a good excuse for him to get it.

Conn took another few steps forward, but Lacey hung back, too stunned by the venomous flow of his stride to move. Her gaze connected with Ashlyn's, and Lacey shook her head sadly.

By now, Connor was face to face with Johann. They were almost matched in height and bulk, coloring and temperament.

"It is about time you told me who you are," said Spencer.

A pause filled the room. Lacey wondered what exactly Conn would say. She'd revealed herself to him today. Would he do the same?

And, Lord help her, Lacey wanted to know the answer to Johann's question more than anyone.

Connor sent a quick glance to Lacey, as if in apology, then turned back to Johann. "Can't you guess who I am? Or are you more of a fool than I thought?"

"I have my theories." Johann tugged his dark coat

around him, almost as if a shiver had zipped down his spine and he was warding off another one.

"So you're not all-knowing." Connor laughed, but without any glee. A sense of anticipation threaded through the room, holding every stiff body in thrall.

"My name's Connor Langley. My real father is Horatio Spencer, and I'm here to claim what's rightly mine."

Oh, God. She hadn't wanted to truly believe it.

Dread pounded Lacey's temples as she looked at Ashlyn again—a stunned, unmoving Ashlyn. Her friend. The woman with whom she should've shared her suspicions. The woman who fully understood the wickedness of the Spencer family and how they could take everything away from you.

Everything like love, pride, an inheritance.

A glass castle.

As Ashlyn clumsily fled the room, hand over mouth, Connor watched her leave, an unreadable expression on his face. But instead of going to his sister, he faced Johann.

With one revealed secret, Connor had switched sides.

He'd become one of Lacey's enemies.

Chapter Ten

"You couldn't have told me who you were right off the bat?" demanded Lacey, hurling her coat and scarf on the mudroom floor as she and Connor entered her house from the garage.

After he had made a silent, grand exit from the ice-cream shop, Lacey had been too tongue-tied to talk to him on their drive home. Instead, she'd chosen to call Ashlyn on her cell phone, asking her best friend if she wanted company after Connor's explosive news. Ashlyn had politely declined Lacey's offer, but Lacey had promised to check on her in a few hours anyway.

After the call, Lacey had gone awkward and silent around Connor. He'd looked so satisfied, so righteous as he drove, she couldn't bring herself to ruin his moment.

After all, he'd gone on to defend her, to tell the town that she wasn't crazy, that he would stand up for her if they blighted her name again.

"I had plans," Connor said, following her out of the mudroom and into a hallway, then the kitchen. He shed his own coat. "I thought it was important that no one knew my identity. I needed time to gather information, to go about this thing with some stealth and cleverness."

"You just blew your cover, Mr. *Spencer.*"

He caught her by the arm, turned her around. "Why are you talking to me like this? I'm the same guy I was an hour ago, out in the stone garden."

"No, you're not." She'd been too upset to confront him in the car, and now it was all coming out in a flood of frustration. "Has it escaped your attention that the Spencer family is trying to rob me of my castle land?"

His voice lowered, and he gentled his hold on her arm. "You know it hasn't. In fact, it's been like an anvil on my conscience."

"And that anvil landed on my friend today." She shook off his grasp, then headed toward the stairs.

As she mounted the steps, boot thumps sounded behind her. "Don't think you can follow me up here," she said. "I'm going to my room and locking the door behind me."

"Aw, Jeez. You're not hearing me out."

"I think I've tolerated enough."

They reached the top landing, and Lacey indeed went straight for her room, securing the door behind her. She could feel him on the other side, probably shaking his head while leaning against the door frame.

Funny. She never could've imagined barring a man like Connor from her bedroom.

"Lacey." His deep voice penetrated the door, reaching through the wood.

She turned toward the inanimate object, finding it much easier to address a faceless slab than Connor himself. "What happened to the good old days when you wanted to be left alone in the forest? Now's your chance to be that hermit."

Silence. Her words must've hit home. Not that the realization made her feel any better.

There was such a long pause Lacey thought she'd definitely scared him away. So what. She'd told him to leave, hadn't she?

She dragged off her boots, tossing them into her walk-in closet, then wiggled out of her warm woolen tights, her socks.

With a certain amount of shame, she recognized this ritual. Back in her pre-HazyLawn days, she used to retreat to her bed in a numb state of depression— sometimes in the middle of the day—only to stare at the walls as sleep evaded her. She'd curl up in a fetal ball, hugging her knees to her stomach, not feeling anything except the lump in her throat. A lump which usually ended up in her chest, right where her heart should've been.

Lacey kicked her tights across the room and turned away from the bed, refusing to groove back into her old habits. Sure, it'd be comfortable; she'd know exactly what to expect.

But the easy promise of chasing away her emotions wouldn't do her a bit of good. She knew that.

She marched toward the door and flung it open. The breath left her body as she saw Connor standing there, just as she'd imagined him—slumped against the door frame. But he wasn't the same as she'd pictured.

He'd buried his face against a forearm, his pale hair hanging like a fall of rain to obscure his features. The strands moved when he spoke.

"I messed it all up, and good. Didn't I?"

He was too near, too big. Lacey's heart stuttered with such fierce panic that she was sure she was about to lose her ability to inhale oxygen.

He continued, his voice muffled. "I never meant to hurt you. I only wanted to help my mom before she got sick again, only wanted to make sure she doesn't ache deep in her bones anymore. I can't watch that happen, no matter what it takes."

She made a small sound of sympathy, drawing aside his hair with her fingers before she could think better of it. "So you don't have much of a choice? Is that what you think?"

"Cash for her treatment doesn't grow like leaves,

not even in Raintree, Montana.'' His smile obviously cost him some effort as it stretched over his lips.

If Lacey hadn't extended her finances with her quixotic glass castle, she would've been able to offer Connor money for his mother's health. She wondered if he'd accept help from the Cassidys—Nick and Meg. There's a family who could manage to give aid.

''I know people who can afford to—''

He cut her off with a look, his head raised from his forearm. ''Horatio Spencer has a responsibility to my mother. He won't go shirking his duty.'' He spoke more to himself than her. ''I still have enough time to make sure of that.''

''It may be that your mother has recovered. Isn't that a possibility?''

''Every time I talk to her on the phone, she assures me she's fine. But I want to be sure she's taken care of, just in case. She deserves it.'' He straightened to his full height, then, as if remembering she was there, he ran a long gaze over her body.

Lacey's breasts tingled, tightened. A powerful warmth stole over the skin of her belly, delving inside of her, stirring up her emotions.

Why did she care so much about Connor's business? He hadn't even been in her life before a few weeks ago.

Lacey stopped herself, realizing she couldn't bear the thought of life before Connor. Her old existence was almost like a neglected painting, the oils covered with time-gathered dust and dirt. Her new life was the same work of art, restored, brought back to vivid colors with some attention and care.

Admit it, she thought. You've been in love with this guy since the minute he stepped into that dilapidated cabin.

It was true. From that first, tense moment, her life had blossomed into more than just a monochromatic snowscape. Her existence had changed hues, spreading into her soul with the soft, sun-kissed palette of a new spring.

As his gaze swept over her sweater, her skirt, down to the tips of her bare toes, Lacey melted a little more each passing second.

"Stop it," she said, too embarrassed about how she'd reacted the last time she'd been this worked up. She wasn't about to make a lust-crazed fool out of herself again. She wasn't about to face rejection.

"Stop what?"

"That…that staring at me."

"All right."

He still seemed so melancholy. How in the world could she think he was anywhere near as bad as the Spencers?

"It puts me on edge," she said.

"You're just…" He smiled wryly. "I'm itching to lay my hands on you again."

Her tummy jumped, rendering her speechless. Maybe he really *didn't* care that she was less than perfect for him. Or maybe he just wanted physical release, and he didn't intend to bring emotional baggage into the equation.

Heck, why couldn't she admit she was as eager to feel him against her no matter the circumstances? Why did she have to be so mortified about the urgency she'd felt the other night, when she'd just about thrown him against the couch and had her way with him?

Incredible. Twenty-seven years old and she had no idea how to make a pass at a man.

He must've mistaken her hesitation for disinterest, because he backed away. "Sorry. I guess my plain speaking should give way to silence once in a while."

"No," she said, blurting out the word. "I hope you don't change, Connor. In fact, I think my heart might break if you do."

It was as if all the invisible supports that had been holding him up throughout his mother's illness had suddenly been stripped away. His shoulders relaxed, and he leaned into her, cupping her jaw with his hands, resting his forehead against hers.

To have him this near, to smell his skin—the earthy scent of wind blowing through strands of sweet hay… She could bask in him forever, couldn't imagine not having him next to her.

Her life would be so empty without him.

With a soft mewling sound that she couldn't keep inside, Lacey lifted her face to his, skimming her lips over his, testing to see if he was as willing to fall into forever as she was.

Oh, yeah. Willing and able.

He responded fervently, the gentle kiss flaming into the urgent thrust of his tongue entering her mouth, tangling with her own. In his passion, he pressed her against the hallway wall, his head hitting one of the Asian-flavored pictures, forcing the metal frame against wood.

She'd adjust it later. Or not. Who cared.

Now, she was too busy shucking off his shirt, feeling the slight scratch of five-o'clock shadow whisk against her cheeks, burning the skin with a languid flush.

Their kiss deepened, becoming one long swirl of lips and gasps. Lacey was ecstatic he wasn't holding back this time, that he seemed as determined to get his fill of her as she was of him.

As she nailed up the back of his neck, coaxing him to get even closer, Lacey slowed down the kiss, leaning into the part of him that was growing harder by the moment, tasting his tongue, then rubbing her lower lip over his.

Thank goodness. Air.

Their breathing was jagged, heartbeats punching at each other through their skin and her sweater, while she rested her head against his shoulder.

"Boy," she said.

"Yeah."

They panted a little more, until he'd obviously suffered through enough of it. Then he guided her backward into her room.

Toward the bed.

A nervous thrill whirled through her. What if she didn't know how to please him? What if she did everything wrong?

If he stopped their lovemaking again, she'd crumble for certain. She'd fall apart because all she wanted to do was make him happy.

The bed hit the back of her knees, and she almost buckled, falling onto the mattress. Connor slipped a brawny arm around her waist, stopping her descent.

"Tell me if this is what you want."

He was kissing her again, jamming all logical frequencies. She wasn't even sure she knew how to talk anymore.

"I want this." There. She'd managed.

"You sure?" He bent down to run his tongue over one throbbing neck vein.

"Mmmm. Yes, I'm sure."

He grazed his teeth over the tender center of her throat, his hair lingering over her skin like a silk scarf, ready to bind her to him.

"I don't want to hurt you," he said. "Not ever."

"Oh, great. The kid-glove treatment again." Her pride wanted to pull away from him, to stubbornly make a point. But her body wouldn't allow it.

"It's not that." He lifted his head from her neck, ran his knuckles over her cheek. "It's just—"

His voice faded, eyes misting over into a dark-blue haze. As he planted kisses on her ear and in the cove behind it, Lacey didn't push him to finish his thoughts. Instead, she fought lightheadedness, the sensation of feeling her earlobes throb in time to her pulse.

Air whooshed on her skin as he lifted her sweater over her head. He used his hands to mold her ribs, used his thumb tip to trace the line traveling from her belly to the waist of her skirt. The contact almost tickled her, but she found herself struggling for breath instead of laughing.

He worked off her skirt, tossing it aside. As she watched it flutter through her room to land on the floor, Lacey clutched Connor's shoulder, enthralled by the rough warmth of his skin.

How many times had she imagined this scenario? Having the man she loved touch her as if she was the only person who mattered, the only one who could bring him to the point where he was flinging skirts across the room.

Now that it was actually happening, it was almost surreal. Unreal. Couldn't be real.

He didn't even pause after he'd gotten rid of the skirt. While it was still settling to a landing, Connor had slipped his hands over Lacey's back, working at her bra. As he eased it off, she couldn't help covering herself, watching the wisp of white lace as he held it in his hands, taking it away from her.

Leaving her open to him.

"Hey," he said softly, allowing the bra to drop to the ground, too. "Let me see you."

The hardened buds of her nipples chafed against

her arms. She'd always been a little ashamed of her small breasts, had always wondered why she'd been cursed to swim in the shallow end of the boob pool. Her mom had evidently gotten the benefit of nature, but not Lacey.

She'd inherited the depression chromosome instead.

When she hesitated, Connor grinned at her. ''You have no idea how perfect you are.''

She watched as he reached out, peeled her arms away from her chest. Instead of disgust or disappointment, his gaze darkened, smoked like the after-burn of an explosion.

He ran his palms over her breasts, shaping them, his fingers circling the crested nubs until Lacey closed her eyes with the heady thrum of her blood pumping down to the center of her legs. He lay her back on the bed, licking one nipple, running his tongue over it, then taking it into his mouth.

Lacey cupped his head, cradling him, threading her fingers through his hair as he sucked and nipped at her. When he fixed his attention on her other breast, she shifted under him, feeling his arousal beat against her leg.

He slid upward, his bare chest brushing against hers. This felt so right, skin on skin, sliding against each other, knowing she was going to burst if he didn't come into her soon.

She swooned upward, rubbing against his hardness,

hearing him mutter a curse as he slipped off her undies.

He nestled his thumb between her damp thighs, stroking the most sensitive place on her body. She felt his fingers slip inside of her, and she couldn't help the accompanying moan.

As he kissed his way up her stomach, Lacey wanted to shout her love for him. But something held her back. Something culled from years of defending herself, barricading herself from the taunts and rejection of others.

Connor removed his weight from her, leaving her feeling bereft while he took off his pants. He searched a back pocket, his wallet, taking out a condom, unwrapping it.

Thank goodness. She never kept protection around. Didn't really have occasion to.

Except now.

He sheathed himself in it, then returned to her, looming over her body as he kissed her again.

"No turning back, Lace."

"That's okay," she said, her voice trembling. Heck, she was quivering all over, as if something was inside, struggling to get out.

He gently spread her knees, prodding against her, then entering with a slick thrust. His length made her hitch a breath because it'd been so long ago....

He stopped, probably because he felt how tight she was. "Lacey?"

She wrapped her legs around his, desire overcoming the discomfort as she urged him forward, rocking against him until he followed her rhythm.

They moved together, bumping into the headboard, tearing sheets off the corners of the bed. But Lacey didn't mind any of it. She was traveling over clouds, riding waves of air, breathing into Connor's neck, feeling the sweat-soaked ends of his hair as they trailed over her skin.

She'd never felt such sensation—deliriously, achingly alive, all of her nerve ends open to pain. And pleasure.

She could spend forever like this, gliding against his skin, feeling him fill her empty places with insistent urgency. She could spend her life spinning like a ballerina into the stars until they showered over the earth, spreading sparks over the rocks of her garden.

The hardness of her resolve.

As he reached a shattering climax, Lacey clutched him to her, never wanting their connection to end. Even as he pleasured her to a second star burst, she held on.

She was afraid to let go.

He'd never felt this way before. Not with his ex-fiancée, not with old girlfriends.

With Lacey, there was a fragile bond. Not that he could explain all this emotional stuff, but there was something more than lust or sex.

Connor watched her sleep, reaching out to trace a finger over her plump, kiss-pinked lips. Her dark hair spread over the white of the pillow, making her seem like a fairy-tale princess who'd been cursed to sleep by a wicked force.

He wondered if another kiss would wake her up.

He tried, and it did.

She smiled at him, blushing as she tugged the sheet up to her neck. Didn't matter much because he could still see the small, beautiful mounds of her breasts outlined by the thin linen.

"Hi," she said.

"Hi."

They paused, gazing at each other. Connor suspected her inexperience. Or maybe she hadn't been with a man in a long time. When he'd been inside her, she'd been so tight, wrapping him in her heat with velvet-slicked comfort.

It must've been on her mind, as well. "You didn't defile me or anything. Just so you know."

"I wanted to make sure it was right for you."

She snuggled into the pillow. "Don't worry. You met all my expectations."

"You haven't been with many…"

"Yeah."

Her blush intensified. God, he'd mattered. He'd passed all her tests and been held in such high esteem that she'd singled him out.

Pressure built up inside his conscience, urged on by an unwelcome four-letter word that started with "L." Why had Lacey chosen him over anyone else?

He had to dissuade her from caring too deeply before he hurt her. "The honor is all mine," he said, meaning it.

She gave him that soft, hair-spread-on-pillow look he'd fantasized about in the stone garden. God, it was happening. Actually, happening.

"Have there been a lot of women for you?" she asked, an undercurrent of doubt in her tone, in spite of its teasing lilt.

He smiled down on her. "I had a fiancée before I came to Kane's Crossing."

That doubt intensified, flashed across her eyes. "Had, not have?"

He couldn't help it. He didn't want to see her wounded, so he touched her, drew a finger over her collarbone until she glowed again.

"She broke off our engagement when I reacted badly to this Spencer issue. See, when the cancer returned, my mom decided to tell me everything. About how she'd fallen in love with Horatio before she met my adoptive dad. About how the very married Horatio had jilted her, leaving her a single mother who had to fend for herself and a baby. He'd known she was pregnant, and he still dumped her. What a hero, huh? That's my real dad for you."

Connor kept stroking her, watching how her gaze widened as he got closer to her breasts. "My adoptive dad, John Langley, married my mom, even though he knew I wasn't his child. And, up until his death, that man raised me as his own. Horatio refused to claim me. John could've hated me, but he didn't, thank goodness. I owe my happiness to him. Unfortunately, he died when I was a teenager, before Mom told me the truth and I could tell him how much I love and respect him for what he did.''

Lacey shuddered as Conn tugged the sheet away from her skin. ''And you're here, in Kane's Crossing, to make sure Horatio's family takes up where he left off?''

He covered her with his body once again, feeling himself stiffen against the moist core of her. ''I'm going to make certain he at least acknowledges my mother, that he gives her back some dignity. If he doesn't have enough honor to do that, then…''

It would make him doubt his own worth as well. Because Connor was a Spencer, too.

Lacey had fetched a condom from his wallet and enfolded him in her hand, then shrouded him with the protection, making Conn gasp with the pleasure of her touch. Softly, so softly he wasn't even sure he heard her, she whispered, ''I love you and your honor, Conn Langley.''

As she guided him into her once again, Connor wished he was indeed a Langley, that he had enough sense of self to make him a whole man.

And that he had the honor she deserved.

Chapter Eleven

That evening, after hours spent in Conn's arms, Lacey held his hand as they walked into Siggy Woods.

They'd bundled into their snow clothes in time to see dusk draping itself over the horizon, burnishing the treetops with silhouette fringes. Conn used a lantern to lead the way through the trees.

When they came upon the cabin, Lacey clasped her hands together. "I can't believe it!"

The structure was restored to most of its former glory, though it still sagged with the same air of craggy ruggedness.

Heck, thought Lacey. You could even say the place resembled an old man who'd gotten himself a spiffy new haircut, with the roof's new wood basking under the waning sunlight.

Conn ambled over to the cabin, one hand stuffed in the pocket of his coat, a certain workman's pride hiding in the curve of his grin as he shone the lantern's light over his accomplishment. "So it meets your approval?"

Everything about him did. The way he'd held her today, the way he'd gazed into her eyes as she'd reached the heights of passion. Lacey still couldn't believe they'd been so intimate.

"Yes, it does. Thank you for all the dedication."

"Don't mention it." He paused. "Has anyone commented on my being out here?"

"No. When Rick got a little suspicious, I told him I'd hired a handyman to fix this place up. Why?"

His brow furrowed, then relaxed. "No reason really. Just… This morning, I thought I saw footprints in a patch of snow by the window, as if someone had been looking inside the cabin. Hell, truth is, someone *was* looking in."

He shrugged, probably in response to Lacey's opened mouth. "Maybe I'm seeing things," he continued, "but I thought I caught an old woman's face in the window. Even though the snow's melted now and there's no sign of her, I can't shake the feeling someone knows I'm here."

Lacey tried to ignore the wariness that had crept over the bumps of her spine. "It was probably some kids running around the woods. We get a lot of troublemakers in these parts. Or maybe it was The Wanderer. She's homeless, but harmless, too."

He stared out the window. "Could be."

Lacey sent him an encouraging smile, then walked closer to the cabin, eyeing the window he'd been referring to. From this spot, she could see his bed, his clothes peeking out of a bag on the floor. Had someone, other than The Wanderer, been spying on him?

"Let's get inside," he said, opening the door and waiting for her to precede him. "I patched up the walls so it's not drafty."

When she entered his domain—she couldn't think of it any other way now—she found he was right. The air was a comfortable temperature. It made her wonder, all the same, if he'd be spending the night here, in the home he'd rebuilt, or with her.

"Conn? What are you going to do next?"

He started a fire, his back to her. Obviously he planned to stay in the cabin for a while tonight.

"I mean," she continued, "your presence is hardly a secret anymore. Plan A has been blown to bits."

He turned, his face in profile. "I guess it's time to lay my cards on the table, to confront Johann and see about contacting Horatio since he isn't in town. I wish I had time to do this right—to identify some of the Spencers' weaknesses and gain the upper hand before rushing in to plead my mother's case. But I suppose that's what lawyers are for. To do the dirty work. I'll wait for them to lead the charge."

"Legalities. That could take forever." And his mother didn't necessarily have a fraction of that luxury.

Conn stood, facing the fire again, bringing back memories of the day Lacey had discovered him in the cabin. Now he belonged here.

Problem was, Connor Langley belonged to the Spencers, also. And his plans to right the wrongs in his life didn't include Lacey.

The thought left her as empty as the top of an hourglass, one that had run out of sand, out of time.

He said, "Part of me wants to make the Spencers pay for what Horatio did to Mom. The other part wonders about my real dad. It wants to see the look on his face when I'm introduced to him."

"Does that portion want him to open his arms to you?"

Finally, Conn left the fire, coming to stand before the window that faced the Spencer estate. "I hate to admit it but, yeah, it does. The thought of being slapped away, ignored again, doesn't sit well."

She knew what he meant. If his real dad rejected him, it would feel a lot like her own mother's treatment of her. He'd be stranded, isolated, even in the middle of a crowd of people who loved him.

"What about the other Spencers?" she asked. "You've got a half sister. Ashlyn."

He smiled, holding out a hand, inviting Lacey to join him at the window. "I haven't forgotten. I'm still in awe of the fact that she exists, but I made a mess of things with her already."

With a sigh of relief, Lacey cuddled into Conn's arms, folding into his strong embrace as if it was a dark cloud that she could hide in for the rest of the night. "She's a forgiving person, artistic, imaginative. You're lucky to have inherited at least her."

"I hope she'll accept me."

All this talk about acceptance was unsettling Lacey, because when Conn finished his business with the Spencers, when he was on his way back to Montana to help his mother, where would that leave her?

She didn't want to think about it. "Ashlyn won't be able to help loving you."

Conn stiffened and, initially, Lacey thought it was because of the "love" reference. She'd accidentally said the word today while they'd made love, but either he hadn't heard her—or he'd avoided the topic.

When she peered up at him, his gaze was fixed on the window. "What is it?" she asked.

He shook his head, his arms dropping from their embrace, leaving Lacey wary.

"Someone's out there right now," he said, his voice low, calm.

Lacey followed his gaze. From the distance, a shape approached the cabin, the beam of a flashlight playing on the ground before it.

With the same maddening ease, Conn opened the door, and Lacey followed, huddling into her jacket for protection.

As the person came closer, Lacey could see it was a little boy. Little Alfie, the son of Magda, the Spencer maid.

The kid's furry snow hat dipped over his eyes as

he came to stand in front of Connor. He held out a creamy white envelope, which Connor accepted.

"Alfie?" asked Lacey. "What are you doing?"

He grinned up at her. "Mr. Spencer said to give the message to the man in the woods, the man living in the cabin."

When had Johann found out Conn was living here? The question sent a quiver of trepidation through her stomach.

As Conn tore open the envelope and scanned the contents, Alfie waved goodbye, then sprinted toward the estate.

For a minute, Conn didn't say a word. He merely watched Lacey with an unreadable expression. Then, he said, "We've been summoned to the Lion's Den."

"What do you mean?"

"A cocktail party, tomorrow, thrown by none other than Johann Spencer."

He crumpled the invitation, backhanding it into the darkness of the cabin.

Even though he'd rejected the entreaty, Lacey knew he'd be there. And she'd darn sure be with him.

The next night, as Lacey readied herself for the Spencer cocktail hour, Conn found himself in the hallway in front of her room once again, staring at the door.

He was light years from yesterday when they'd made love in there. Today, he was standing on the edge of a precipice, wobbling between two identities, two needs.

On one hand, he wanted to stay a Langley, through and through. On the other, he wanted security for his mother, wanted to be accepted by the family who should've recognized him long ago.

He hated himself for craving a sign of compassion—of anything—from his real father.

Conn stared at the wall, at the picture hanging on a crooked angle. Memory assaulted him: pressing Lacey to the wood with such passion he'd hit the frame with his head, knocking it askew.

He shouldn't have taken advantage of her like he had, not knowing where he'd be next week much less the next hour. His whole life could change at this cocktail party, and where would that leave Lacey?

Would he be part of *that* family?

With another curse, he righted the picture just as Lacey opened her door.

The first thing that struck him was the crushed-blue of her gaze while she watched him touch the reminder from yesterday. A reminder that he hadn't spent last night in her bed because he felt so guilty about the possibility of hurting her.

The second thing that hit him was the flowing buttercup sheerness of her dress, and how the wispy material misted over her shoulders, her waist, her legs to evoke the tragic beauty of a princess locked in a tower.

He couldn't say anything for a second.

"What's wrong?" she asked.

Conn dropped his hands to his sides. "You've always been so beautiful but, right now, it's painful to look at you."

She literally stepped back, hand flying to her throat. "Thank you, Connor."

This was one of those times that he wished he knew how to hold his tongue, to be a little more diplomatic and elusive. Damn his country-boy urge to be plain-spoken.

"Yeah, well," he said.

Lacey's hand drifted up to her hair, where a few curls fought to stay corkscrewed. Already they were wilting, softening her features more than he thought possible, making her eyes more doelike, her lips more full and vulnerable.

"You know what to say to a girl. Don't you?"

"Not too often." Awkwardly, he made one attempt, two, to offer her his arm. Just like a gentleman would, he hoped.

She accepted the gesture, smiling at him, making Conn want to wrap her in his arms and never let go. They stepped down the stairs, her long dress trailing after them like a brocaded veil.

As he helped her into a heavy shawl, a Spencer town car pulled into Lacey's driveway. He shrugged into his own coat and led her outside.

In spite of the Spencers living on the other side of the woods, Johann had offered a ride. Though cautious about the kindness, Conn recognized the need to arrive in style, without having to traipse through the trees and over damp ground.

The ride flew by in a whir of winter-bare trees and starlight. Before Conn knew it, he and Lacey were shedding their coat and shawl and being offered champagne before following the butler through the Italian-marbled foyer and into a larger area.

The same marble decorated the mantel of the fireplace and the corners of the room. Delicate fleur-delis etchings trimmed the walls, the pattern reflected in the thick carpeting. As a string quartet eked out classical standards, caterers stood sentinel over steaming buffet tables filled with appetizers that didn't look fit to feed a fly.

Nonetheless, Conn couldn't help being impressed. Or maybe *seduced* was a more appropriate term.

This wealth reflected his family, his means to make his mother safe from another round of cancer.

Conn scanned the crowd, which mainly consisted of the black-garbed, silk-tied crème de la crème of society, until he found Johann. He was surrounded by enthralled women, except for one female. Was the lady with the been-there-done-that expression Johann's wife?

"Welcome to Spencer World," said Lacey, a polite smile fixed on her mouth, "the most delusional place on earth."

"This is an E ticket, all right." Conn fingered one of Lacey's withered curls. "You look as if you belong in a house like this. You're comfortable."

"It's the art of schmoozing. Business people are really good at it. Which reminds me. I've got an important conference call tomorrow—"

He placed his finger over her lips, and Lacey closed her eyes.

"Don't think about it."

For a moment, she seemed lost in his touch. He couldn't believe he had that sort of effect on a woman, especially one as independent and beautiful as Lacey. To think, a Montana boy being able to win the love of a successful lady like her....

A cultured voice interrupted them. "Connor, Lacey."

Johann. Face-to-face, it was almost like peering into a still body of water, sudden ripples distorting Conn's image as it mirrored back at him.

Lacey metamorphasized back into the business woman he'd first met. "Are we on a first name basis, Mr. Spencer? Or are you making assumptions again? Because you know what they say when we *assume*..."

Conn grinned at her feistiness.

Johann's wife, garbed in mink and silk, slid up to her husband, saying, "When you assume, you make a *donkey* out of *you* and *me*. You see, on the continent, we watched repeats of *The Odd Couple,* as well."

She seemed much too smart to be wed to Johann. Conn wondered how she'd been cursed by such bad luck.

Johann shook his head. "My wife Anna does not quote it correctly. It was not a donkey to which they were referring. It was an a—"

Lacey shot Conn a miffed look that said, "Are we here to argue about Oscar and Felix?"

"At any rate," continued Anna, "I am sure Ms. Vedae is as bored of you as I am, Johann." She addressed Lacey. "Come talk girl issues with me."

Another glance, this one asking if Conn wanted to be left alone with Johann. The set up was obvious.

Conn nodded slightly, accompanying the gesture with an overconfident grin. This was the moment he'd been waiting for—and dreading—ever since he'd learned the truth of his parentage. He wanted to meet it head on, take care of the situation like a man should.

Did he imagine it or did Lacey's mouth quirk with concern, even a degree?

It happened too quickly to know for sure, and she'd left with Anna before he could get a second glance.

Then he was alone with the man who was the key to his mother's future.

"Come to my study, Connor," said Johann, friendly as could be. "I have many polo trophies there."

"Polo." Damn. Great first words.

"Yes. Horses, mallets..."

"I know what polo is, Johann."

"Then there it is." The man led him away from the latest violin/cello arrangement and the smells of lobster. They ended up in a first-floor room which was indeed decorated with golden statues of accomplishment.

Johann didn't even bother to talk about polo anymore. "I did not know if you would accept my invitation. I am happy to have you in my home."

My home. The jerk knew he was playing with semantics. This home had once belonged to Connor's biological father.

When Conn didn't say anything, the other man smiled grimly. "You realize all this splendor could have been yours if Horatio had only avoided getting caught."

"The man's a criminal." There. It felt good to say it. It hurt to say it.

"The man is your father."

Shock sparked through Conn. Johann was admitting it?

"Do not seem surprised at my willingness to voice the connection. Any fool can see you are a Spencer, merely by glancing at you. If you like, I will contact Horatio in Europe to request that he comply with a DNA test, to make matters official."

Shouldn't this be harder? thought Conn.

"Though," added Johann, "I am not sure what good a test will do if you are after the Spencer estate or money. There is no more Spencer fortune as far as your branch of the family is concerned. It is gone. *Poof,* as you might say. This house was rescued with my own capital. So, I am afraid you have no claim to it.''

Conn almost asked Johann to repeat himself. The words weren't getting through. ''Horatio is broke?''

''He is under the care of the European Spencers, clawing his way out from the grave he dug for himself and his family. Be happy you did not get caught with him, like his other son, Chad.''

''I thought…'' No, he wouldn't say it. Not to Johann.

He'd thought that maybe, *maybe,* there would still be some money left, even enough to help his mother, to repair her pride and her body.

But there was nothing.

Johann raised a brow at Conn's devastated expression. ''I am sorry your fortune hunting has come to a close.''

Arrogant idiot. ''I don't want your damned Spencer money.''

''But, yes, you do. I have done my research, just as you have.''

''I see. You sent someone into the woods to spy on me?''

''Yes, it is true.'' Johann spread out his hands in an innocent gesture. ''One of my employees confirmed my suspicion last night. Usually we do not worry about that cabin. There are always Kane's Crossing children running about, getting into mischief. These American kids.''

As if fully spent by the thought, Johann sighed and

settled himself on a leather couch, then motioned for Conn to do the same.

He remained standing.

Johann didn't seem to mind. "I also know about Seonaid. Her cancer. I am sorry to hear this."

What was left to do for his mother? Was she going to die if the cancer returned?

The injustice of it all stabbed through Conn's gut, making him want to take a few of Johann's trophies and club every inch of cabinet glass in the room.

"You haven't much to say," said Johann.

Though Conn tried to control himself, his voice shook. "What the hell am I supposed to say?"

The older man leaned back, considering Conn. "Your mother means the world to you, as does my own family."

Conn couldn't deny it. "Of course."

"I see Lacey Vedae means quite a bit to you, as well."

A protective heat started to burn low in Conn's belly. "What about it?"

Johann's blue eyes flashed with…what was it? Victory? But a triumph over what?

"You have—how to put this—a say with her?"

Conn knew exactly where this was going. A glass castle for his mother's health.

A devil's trade.

His hands fisted, pain flashing in his palms.

"Connor, we have had much discussion with the

Spencer relations about this. We want to welcome you to our family."

The part of him that screamed for acceptance tumbled over itself with jubilant celebration. He wasn't going to be turned away.

Johann leaned forward now, clearly aware he had Conn in hand. "I can see to it you are flown to Europe to meet your father. He cannot come back to the States, you understand, or he will be prosecuted."

Dammit a million times. Why did Conn feel such a need to see his father, a criminal? John Langley forgive him, but he wanted so badly to belong, to bring his mother into the fold.

"And," said Johann, "we will take care of Seonaid. She is the mother of a Spencer child, and you will never have to worry about her health again."

Too much. How could he say no to keeping his mother free from the agony of a disease that ate away at her body, bit by bit?

At the same time, how could he possibly betray Lacey? Destroy the one thing she'd sunk her heart and finances into?

Conn's shoulders slumped under the weight of the bargain.

"What do you want me to do?" he asked.

Even from the other side of the room, he could feel Johann's smile.

Chapter Twelve

"And after Anna finished recapping every *Odd Couple* episode ever made, she launched into *Laverne & Shirley*."

Lacey finished her tirade by holding her head in her hands, shaking it as if her skull would fly off. Anna had driven her to distraction tonight.

They'd arrived back at her kitchen, having finished with the party as soon as Conn came storming down the Spencers' hall to fetch Lacey from Anna's verbal grasp. He'd seemed angry enough to tear down the Spencer estate as they'd jumped into a waiting town car, but he hadn't explained the reason for his mood yet.

Give him time, thought Lacey, as she whipped up

a quick plate for a snack. Homemade taro chips with marinated vegetables lining a main course of panini sandwiches with smoked bacon, baby field greens and basil pesto spread.

What could she say? Cooking kept her mind off Conn's dark demeanor.

She peeked over at him once again. He was reclining on a bar stool, resting his arms on the counter while watching her slice carrots at her island chopping block.

"There's a change in you," she said.

"Not really." He didn't meet her gaze.

She laid down her knife carefully, lining it up with the whole carrots as she spoke. "If you don't want to tell me what Johann said, you don't have to."

"I…" He paused, fisting his hands. "He welcomed me to the family."

What? "Well. That's the last thing I expected you to tell me."

"Johann sat on his leather couch, calm as the dawn, and offered to bring me into the family fold." He stopped, his mouth a grim line.

"That's great. They'll help you with your mother's medical expenses?"

"Yeah, he offered that much."

Words were missing, thought Lacey. He wasn't telling her everything. She could feel it.

He stood, hands shoved under his arms as if to ward off whatever it was that bothered him. "I thought this is what I wanted. To be accepted, to have the Spencers admit Mom is part of their family. But you know what they say, right? Be careful what you wish for.''

''What do you mean?'' Lacey went to him, touched his arm with her fingertips.

He stiffened, and she knew he wasn't going to tell her more than he had to. The realization dragged her down into that black abyss that had been waiting patiently all these years for her to come back to it.

She called on all her strength, willing away the sense of rejection.

Finally, Conn met her gaze, his blue eyes iced over. ''The things Johann told me aren't important enough to repeat.''

''Are you trying to convince yourself or me?''

He flinched, and she removed her hand from his arm. After a cold second, he reached out to hold her fingers in his palm, enfolding them, putting a little faith back into her dashed hopes.

''Whatever happens,'' he said, ''know I care for you. Know I want what's best for my mom, and I'm not only talking about her survival, but her pride. She fell in love with a man who made her a black sheep, who tossed her away after he'd used her. I guess I'm sort of like the heir to her status in the family, but that's not what matters. Erasing her pain is the most important thing in the world to me.''

''I understand.'' Lacey couldn't help thinking this detailed speech was the prelude to something she didn't want to hear.

Hadn't she told herself Conn wouldn't fall in love with a woman like her?

"Connor?" She raised his hand to her lips, rubbed her mouth against his knuckles. She felt a shudder tear through his body.

His body. It could tell her everything he wouldn't say out loud. Couldn't it?

She drew her other hand up his chest, her fingers toying with the buttons on his shirt. Peeking at him from beneath her lashes, Lacey knew this might be her most important negotiation to date.

Indecision warred in his irises—soft blue beating back crystalline spears of ambition. Finally, he bent his head to hers, closing his eyes.

"What the hell am I going to do?" he asked, his voice strangled.

Lacey rubbed her nose against his cheek, the burn of new stubble heating her skin. "You'll do the right thing. You're that kind of man."

He clasped his arms around her. His bulk, his taut muscles, his warmth all made Lacey safe. Nothing bad could touch her now.

"And that's why I love you," she whispered before she could think about what she was saying.

Conn expelled a deep breath, as if a heavy weight had suddenly crushed his chest. The air stirred the withered curls near Lacey's ears, tickling them like empty promises.

"If I could," he said, "I'd want to fall in love with a woman just like you."

And there it was.

Cold shock sucked out her insides, left her a hollow shell. But she tried to remain strong on the outside, as she'd done every year since HazyLawn.

God, she wanted to hide.

"Don't worry," she said, smiling against his chest, shutting her eyes before emotion could betray her. "You're going to fall in love with me whether you like it or not."

They stood in silence for what seemed like hours, with him holding her. Then, she led him to her bedroom for the second time that week.

For the rest of the night, she tried to tell herself that being held in his arms was the best they could manage right now.

But it wasn't much of a consolation prize.

The next afternoon, after Lacey had taken care of her conference call and other assorted business, she stood before Conn, hands on hips, as he sat on the couch.

"You heard me," she said.

"No." He leaned back, finding it hard to even meet her gaze. He'd hurt her last night, God help him. He hadn't meant to. "I'm *not* sure I heard you right. Ashlyn is here? Now?"

A knock sounded on the front door, echoing Conn's escalated heartbeat.

"She called earlier today, finally willing to meet with you. It took her some time, but she's ready now.'' Lacey removed her hands from her hips. ''Don't give her any more grief than she's already had to bear.''

Conn almost asked, ''What do you think I am?'' But he knew the answer. Yeah. He was the worst of mankind.

Last night, after Johann had made his offer, Conn had tormented himself, cursing himself for making his relative think he'd consider selling out Lacey for the sake of his mother.

But wasn't that what he'd do? Sacrifice this woman's happiness?

The rational side of him stepped up. What the hell kind of choice did he have? His mother might fall to cancer if it returned to strip away her health. And the family was willing to recognize her. That was the most important part, really, the regained honor. The fact that his mom—in life or in death—would be embraced, redeemed, by the people who had spurned her.

Lacey watched him, shot him a wary glance, probably a remnant from last night's rejection of her love, then went to answer the door. After the lull of female voices greeting each other, she and Ashlyn entered the living room.

His half sister stared at him, biting her lip, her eyes gentled by a sheen of unshed tears. Her hands rested on a belly that seemed ready to pop open at any moment. Lacey receded into the background, probably thinking she was in the way.

Conn hoped he hadn't been the one to make her feel so insignificant.

He sent a slow smile to Lacey, receiving one back. A cautious, hopeful one. Then, he stood in front of his half sister, awkwardly fisting his hands at his sides. "Maybe you shouldn't be on your feet."

A combination hiccup and sob was Ashlyn's answer. "I put off this meeting as long as I could, but I know it's inevitable."

He walked closer. "I mean it. You look ready to give birth at any…"

She drifted to him, hugging him, accepting him. Slowly, he allowed himself to embrace her, too, patting her back when he felt tears staining his shirt.

Out of the corner of his eye, he saw Lacey fade out of the room. "No," he said to her. "Stay. Please."

She nodded, sitting in a nearby chair.

Thank goodness she hadn't argued with him. He didn't think he could talk around the lump in his throat.

The hug lasted for a short eternity, almost as if he and Ashlyn were making up for all the years they hadn't known each other existed.

Finally, she pulled back, wiping at her nose. "You're a fine hanky, Connor."

He fetched some tissue, still unable to speak. This was his sister, something he'd always wanted. Once, when he was very young, he'd asked his parents why they didn't give him a little sibling. They'd merely traded uncomfortable glances, and John had blushed to the roots of his hair.

"Sometimes God puts all the good things in one basket," he'd said.

It'd taken Connor years to realize that John had meant Connor. And he was pretty sure his adoptive father and his mother weren't able to have kids together.

That made Ashlyn a miracle in Connor's eyes.

He led his sister to a chair, making sure to elevate her feet.

"You're more of a mother hen than Sam is," she said. "I swear, my husband won't stop clucking over me."

Lacey spoke up. "Do I hear you complaining?"

"No." Ashlyn smiled, eyes sparkling as she fixed her gaze on Connor, who'd by now sat on the footstool next to her. "I can't believe I have a brother. A *real* brother. Chad was never much of one."

Conn wondered if Chad was anything like Horatio or Johann, sly and clever, bargaining lives with ease. "What do you mean, a real brother?"

Ashlyn settled back, trading glances with Lacey, who stood from her chair.

"I'm going to fix coffee and tea while you two hash it out." Then she left the room.

Conn watched after her, appreciating her petite grace, the way she swept across the length of a room. He was a fool, having told her he couldn't fall in love.

Just because his real father was a cad, did that mean he'd inherited the problem, too?

"I'm so happy you're crazy about her," said Ashlyn.

The words cuffed Conn across the face, nudging his head to meet Ashlyn's stare. "I'm grateful she took me in. She's a good friend."

Ashlyn sighed. "Men. Does someone have to hit you over the head with a heavy blunt object to knock some sense into you?"

He really didn't want to talk about this. "Just tell me about our family. Would you do that?"

A cloud seemed to drift across Ashlyn's features as she hesitated, glancing in the direction of Lacey's exit. Then, finally, she started from the beginning, telling him about her childhood, the way she'd been treated as if she wasn't wanted, the infamous Kane's Crossing cave-in and how the emergency workers could only save her or Chad before the entire cave crumbled. Even though the rock formation had ultimately remained standing, Horatio and Edwina Spencer had chosen the golden Chad over her when it had come right down to it.

He'd read about the episode during his research, but her side of the story revealed a much uglier slant. "They would've forfeited your life?" asked Connor.

Ashlyn nodded. "The cave-in led to a very complicated household. I made my father pay for that decision by becoming quite the wild child. He let me get away with my behavior, too, almost as if taking the punishment. Knowing that my parents loved Chad more than they did me put a strain on the family. I've never felt like I was a part of one, really.''

She smiled at Conn, as if asking if she could start over with him. He took her hand, squeezing it. In the background, he heard a faint knock at the kitchen door, heard Lacey open it. Low voices. Silence.

Ashlyn squeezed his hand right back. ''We've got a lot of catching up to do.''

He could only nod.

They started to talk about his life, his mother, the cancer. They'd only scratched the surface of the story when Lacey entered the room again, tea tray in hands.

She wasn't alone.

An old woman trailed behind her. She wore an outfit composed of black, tattered rags arranged like a cocoon around her thin body. Her craggy, weather-chinked face was lined by wispy, white hair, reminding Conn of snow dusting the face of a rock-strewn hill.

He'd seen her face looking in his window.

As if nothing was out of the ordinary, Lacey set down her goodies and gestured for the old woman to take a seat on the couch. Lacey sat next to her, calmly pouring the hot beverages.

Conn shot a look to Ashlyn, who seemed equally perplexed.

''Ah, Lacey?'' asked his sister, nodding to the guest.

The elderly woman silently greeted Conn and Ashlyn as Lacey gave her the tea, then glanced up. "I take it you both feel comfortable with each other?"

Brother and sister nodded.

What was she up to?

As she arranged something to drink for everyone, Lacey spoke, her businesswoman efficiency clear. "Would you like to introduce yourself?" she asked the old woman.

The lady gave a slow nod, sipped her tea. "I guess the folks around here call me The Wanderer. I live near the woods. Don't get out much, except when Ms. Lacey here gives me her good home cooking. Can't resist that."

"You couldn't resist peeking in my cabin, either," said Conn. He didn't chide the woman, though he hadn't exactly been ecstatic about being spied on, either.

A chipped-tooth, hole-ridden grin answered him. "I knew you were a Spencer before you proclaimed it to the town. Just wanted to be sure of it."

He caught Lacey watching him, apparent longing in her gaze. Conn tried to ignore the way her yearning dug into his skin, demanding a response.

The further he got into Spencer-hood, the more he'd hurt her.

"Your voice," said Ashlyn, leaning forward in her chair. "It sounds…like a children's story." Her brow furrowed and she shook her head. "That's an odd thought."

The old woman set down her tea cup and saucer. "Child, you know me. Reach back into your mind."

Ashlyn shut her eyes. "I can't grasp it."

"You," said the woman, addressing Conn. "You never had a chance with the Spencers. They did your mother wrong."

"Mrs. Clyde?" Ashlyn held her distended stomach, causing Conn to lean toward her, worried that she'd go into labor or whatever it was women did when they were pregnant and upset.

Another smile from the old woman. "Yes, Ashlyn. You remember those bedtime stories I used to read to you, the walks we'd take."

A nanny? Conn saw the woman in a new light. Beneath the rags she hid a normal life—one in which she'd probably worn aprons and button-down coats. One in which she'd smiled with all her teeth, had looked in the mirror to see rosy cheeks from the nippy wind felt during those walks.

"You took care of Ashlyn?" he asked.

Lacey refilled Mrs. Clyde's cup. "Yes. She only bothered to tell me today. Right, ma'm?"

"Didn't see the need," said the woman, gulping down another helping before speaking again. "I hear the gossip in this town, so when I saw Ms. Ashlyn's car in your driveway today, I knew what was happening. Young Connor, here, has been searching for some answers, according to the grapevine. I've got a few of them."

"Ashlyn," asked Lacey. "Are you up for this?"

Conn switched his gaze over to the woman he'd made love with merely days ago. She was so beautiful, so soft with her hair turned up at the ends, with her compassionate eyes fastened on her best friend.

God, how could he even be thinking about Lacey and his libido when his life was being turned upside down? Emily Webster had broken off their engagement because he couldn't devote his time to her and his altered existence. Why had he even thought he could manage to beat the inevitable with Lacey?

His sister nodded in response to Lacey's question. There was a fire in her eyes, an obvious need to know what Mrs. Clyde had come out of hiding for.

Everyone settled back in their seats as the woman began her story.

"I was hired to take care of Chad and, let me tell you, that crazy baby made me earn my paycheck. Spoiled rotten, he was. Edwina and Horatio fought like cats and dogs over how to raise him. She thought he should be treated like the crown prince, while Horatio thought some discipline should be applied. I sided with him, if I can say so now. Not that my opinion matters though.

"Those two grew to detest each other. I could tell by the way they wouldn't talk at meals, by the way they moved into separate bedrooms. Eventually, Horatio started taking long business trips, if you catch my meaning. Started looking elsewhere for some affection, since that cold woman at home couldn't provide it, begging your pardon, Ms. Ashlyn."

Conn's sister merely nodded. "You're not telling me anything new. It's hard to love someone like that."

Conn covered Ashlyn's hand, feeling almost embarrassed at Lacey's melancholy smile as she watched them.

Why should her approval matter so much? Why couldn't he just concentrate on what was unfolding?

Mrs. Clyde continued. "When he came back from one of those trips, Edwina let him have it. And good. The servants were in the pantry one night because there you could hear everything that was said in the Mrs.'s bedroom. She screamed at Horatio about 'that low-born trash' and 'that Irish woman.' My family came through Ellis Island from Ireland, so I took offense to that."

"My mother's parents were Irish," said Conn, steel in his voice.

"Good stock," said Mrs. Clyde with a smile. "Everyone in that household knew Horatio was head over heels for this woman. Seonaid was her name. He threatened to leave the Mrs., even." Here, the old woman laughed, but without a trace of humor. "Edwina didn't take him seriously. Horatio was nothing without her. She was the Spencer mastermind, the woman behind the man. He'd done something illegal during a business deal, and she held all the cards. Told him she'd turn him in if he caused a scandal by leaving her for another woman. A pregnant woman."

A jolt shook Conn. He'd been that baby.

He could feel Lacey's sympathetic gaze on him, but he didn't dare meet it. Didn't dare fall into the temptation she offered.

"So," said Mrs. Clyde, "Horatio gave in to Edwina. She had him by the zipper of his pants. He cut off all communication with the mysterious Seonaid. Never heard from her again. But Horatio struck back at his wife eventually, got her pregnant with Ashlyn here, and she never forgave him. The birth of Chad had been enough."

Ashlyn's chin fell against her chest, moving Conn to comfort her. Lacey came over to sit on the chair's arm and stroke Ashlyn's pixie-styled hair. During the silence, their hands met, brushing skin, sending a quiver of desire, of remembered caresses, through Conn's lower stomach.

Ashlyn murmured, "I should've guessed."

"Oh, honey," said Lacey. She held up her friend, a guardian against the memories.

"If it's of any consequence," said Mrs. Clyde, "the household staff loved you to pieces. We all said, 'If I have a child, I want her to be just like Ashlyn.' Then came the cave-in. I was dismissed at that point, when you were a seven-year-old pup, went off to live with my daughter until I came back here." She paused, a light in her eyes. "You just can't beat the sunsets in Kane's Crossing."

"Mrs. Clyde," said Lacey. "Where do you stay?"

"It's no matter. I'm comfortable. A bit eccentric,

maybe, but I'm free enough to come and go as I please. Don't worry about me, ma'm.''

"I do worry." Lacey rose from her seat, casting a glance at Ashlyn. At Conn.

"I worry about all of you," she said.

Conn looked away, unable to match up to her innocence, her open heart.

She clearly wanted to help him, to be a part of his life, and he couldn't even tell her what he'd agreed to with Johann.

He didn't deserve her. Not anymore.

Chapter Thirteen

Before Ashlyn had left last night, she'd warned Conn about getting involved with the Spencers—Johann in particular.

"You think my parents were bad news," she'd said as Conn walked her to the car. "You just wait until you tangle with the European branch of the family."

Of course, he hadn't told her about Johann's deal.

He'd gone back to the cabin, needing time to himself, time to think about a method that would circumvent the need to betray Lacey.

He'd drawn a blank.

Even the next day, while Lacey had spent her time in her Louisville office, he'd come up empty.

On the third day, early in the morning, he received

another summons from Johann to visit the house. Right away.

What was he, a lackey to be called upon when it was convenient for the family?

But curiosity had gotten the better of him, and he'd tramped over to the Spencer estate, his guard up.

The butler escorted him up the stairs without any greetings from Johann or Anna. He led Connor to a second-story bedroom.

The servant opened the door to a darkened area furnished with pendulous damask curtains framing the windows and hanging over a large four-poster bed. Mahogany trimmed the heavy furniture, lending a gothic air to the rose-scented surroundings.

It took a moment for his eyes to adjust, for the butler to shut the door softly behind him.

"Connor?"

That voice. One that had crooned lullabies in his ear, had soothed him while cool hands had bandaged his scraped knees, had cheered him on when he'd hit home runs into fields that stretched far into the horizon.

His words caught on the edge of surprise. "Mom?"

A frail shape emerged from one of the upholstered chairs. Cotton puffs of white hair clouded out from her shadow, hair that had grown back from a bout with chemotherapy.

"Connor," she repeated. Two slim, gnarled, shadowed arms reached out to him.

"What're you doing here?" He rushed over to her,

gently enveloping her in his embrace. "You didn't mention travel when I talked to you yesterday morning. You should be back in Raintree."

"It is odd, isn't it?" Seonaid pulled back to inspect him with her crisp-blue eyes. "Look at you. Same strong boy as when you left to slay dragons."

Damn. The only thing he'd slayed was Lacey's feelings. The proof of that had hit him full force the night before last when he'd left her alone and she'd watched him return to the woods from her door, hugging herself as if she could ward off an inner chill.

Even when he'd entered the sheltering veil of the trees and he'd again turned toward the house, she'd still been there, the light from the door haloing her body.

He'd almost gone back, but thought better of it.

"Hey," he said. "I asked you what's going on."

Seonaid withdrew from him to sit back in her chair. The dark velvet upholstery all but swallowed her. "Let me sit for a moment," she said, her tone breathy.

Warning bells immediately rang in Conn's mind. "Are you exhausted? Have you seen the doctor lately?"

She held up a hand. "The only thing making me tired is all your questions. And it was a long travel day with that layover at the Denver airport. Nothing more."

Conn couldn't stop a sigh of relief from escaping him as he sat on the bed, listening.

"Your Aunt Trudy harped on me to stay home—she's as pesky as you are, Connor..." Seonaid grinned, leaning forward to stroke his cheek. "But Johann Spencer made quick arrangements, sent a nurse to accompany me on the plane, and Trudy couldn't find an argument to stand against *that.* As we speak, I suppose my helpful Phisoderm Angel is lingering down the hall, waiting for me to give up the ghost."

"I'll never get used to your gallows humor."

She gave his cheek a final pinch and settled back again. "It's the only way I can deal with the threat of what I have honey."

The words halted all motion in the room. Even Conn's blood seemed to stop pumping.

Cancer. The real enemy.

Speaking of which...

"So Johann brought you here." He should've sounded happy, but he knew the older man hadn't been acting out of the kindness of his Good Samaritan's soul. The Spencer patriarch had something up his sleeve.

"Funny, isn't it?" said Seonaid. "All of a sudden he reaches out a helping hand to a fallen woman. I came here out of curiosity. And to be with you."

"He's using us both." Finally. He'd admitted it.

"I know. He's already given me the entire 'welcome to our family' speech. Told me how you're going to take back the Spencers' land." She stared at him with a perception only a mother could cultivate. "Are you willing to accommodate him?"

Connor's gaze combed over his mother, noting the baby's breath texture of her hair. Once it'd been thick and long enough to pull into a rope-strong braid. Now, after her chemo treatments, it had grown back different. Weaker.

"Your life is worth everything to me," he said, while trying not to picture Lacey standing under the glow of her glass castle. How could he help them both?

"No, it's not." With a strength he hadn't seen in years, his mother bolted forward in her chair. "I've lived for sixty-two years now. My life has been all I could've ever wanted. And more, too. Not everyone can claim they've had a husband who loved them beyond measure, or a son who'd give up his soul for them. I'm complete. Do you understand that? I'm content."

Conn's blood raged under his skin, making the hair on his scalp bristle. "You're content to be puppeted by the family of a man who wronged you?"

Seonaid's face took on a pained sadness, almost as if she was back to receiving her chemo treatments. Back to the days when she'd endured the burning, the agony shooting through her fingers, her toes.

He wasn't about to see her suffer again.

She said, "Maybe I never should've told you about Horatio. You haven't been the same since."

"What are you saying? That I have more of a problem with the Spencers than you do?"

"Yes."

The breath stung his lungs, unable to escape. Was she right?

She continued. "I loved John Langley with all my heart. John was ten times the man Horatio was. I wasn't much more than a kid when we were together, my eyes full of stars and daydreams. Horatio was rich, able to take me to fancy restaurants and drive me around in limousines. Believe me, I got past all that when I found out he was married.

"John Langley, the man I consider to be your real father, was the best thing that ever happened to me. Us. He was so secure in himself that he married a woman who was pregnant with another man's child. That's love, Connor. That's a real man for you."

Her forgiveness didn't sit well with Conn. It was too easy. "You don't believe in making Horatio live up to his mistakes?"

Seonaid shook her head. "My life is the best revenge possible. I have no regrets. When I told you about your biological father, I was in so much pain I thought I was dying. Then the pain passed, just like this will for you."

Conn stood, pacing the room. "And what if the sickness returns? What then? Who's going to pay?"

The questions didn't need answers. Horatio—the father he despised and wanted to know all at the same time—needed to settle his accounts.

"We'll manage."

She stayed silent, probably knowing Conn would eventually simmer down and listen to reason.

When he did—for the most part—she spoke again. "I know you're curious about your 'other family,' and I'm fine with that. John would've been, too. But remember, Connor, you're a Langley, no matter what your blood says. Live up to John Langley's good name. Live up to our dreams for you."

God, he wanted to make his adoptive father proud. And, with a start, he realized the underlying reason he'd gone in search of Horatio Spencer: he wanted to show the man that Connor Langley was better for not being raised by him.

He paused, collecting himself. "You know," he said, his voice softening, "I met my half sister already. Ashlyn. I think you'd like her a lot." He told his mother about his relationship with his newfound sibling.

"I'd love to meet her someday." Seonaid's eyes focused on a thin stream of light wiggling itself through a crack in the curtains. "But tell me about this girl with the glass castle."

Conn's spine stiffened. He hated when his mother was so sharp. She'd realized that Emily Webster had fallen out of love with him before he'd even had a clue.

"Lacey's real nice," he said cautiously. "Johann obviously told you all about her glass castle and the fact it's housed on the land the Spencers used to own.''

''Yes. Johann might've brought me here to convince you to take part in his plan to get that land back, but I've had enough talk of tourist attractions for one day. I want to know about this Lacey Vedae. Is she…?''

No, screamed his conscience. *No, she's not my girl-friend, or fiancée, or…*

Or what? His lover?

He wasn't dense enough to think he could get away with denying that.

''You've got that touchy attitude men have when they don't want to admit something,'' said Seonaid. ''I think you've got some feelings for this woman.''

''I don't want to talk about it.''

''Of course not, you stubborn oaf. And I say that with all the affection in the world.'' Seonaid ran a hand over her forehead, yawning.

Conn took this as his cue to leave. His mom had already accomplished her agenda, given him an ear-ful.

Though probably not the earful Johann had antic-ipated.

''I'm glad you're here, Mom.''

''Me, too. Now scram. I'll see you soon.''

''I'll get you set up in a motel, just so…''

Just so what? She didn't have to stay with the Spencers? Weren't they part of the family now?

She closed her eyes and nestled into the chair.

"Don't worry about me. I'm living the high life. Who would've ever pictured Seonaid Langley languishing in a mansion?"

Her cavalier statement didn't comfort him. As he pressed a kiss to his mom's temple, covering her with a nearby chenille blanket, Conn tried to put two and two together.

He was sure Johann hadn't flown Seonaid here to have her talk him into betraying Lacey. The wily old fox knew that her haggard appearance, the reminder that death was breathing down her neck, would do the trick without any words.

As Conn gently shut the door on his way out, he swallowed back his disappointment in himself.

Because Johann's gamble had worked.

Unfortunately for Conn, Johann caught him as he was crossing the foyer to exit the mansion.

"A surprise guest?" said the older man with a smug grin. Today he was dressed in silk threads from head to toe, the sun streaming through the windows to lend a blinding sheen to his golden hair.

Conn tried to remain stone faced. "This is a new low, even for you."

"What?" Johann seemed concerned. "Excuse me. I thought it was a grand gesture, a hearty welcome into the Spencer family. She now has a nurse to look after her, as well. Does that not offer more comfort?"

Actually, it did, not that Conn was about to admit it.

"And," continued the older man, "I am making

arrangements for you to see Horatio in Europe. How about that? You can meet in Rome, perhaps? Have you ever tasted gelato under the grandeur of the Trevi Fountain?''

Conn tried valiantly to hold on to the thought of John Langley, tried to superimpose his face over the newspaper photos he'd seen of Horatio Spencer.

The need to appease his longings, to meet the part of him he'd been missing ever since his mother had told him about his real dad, won out.

He'd always love and honor John Langley, but he had to come face to face with Horatio. He wouldn't rest until it was done.

He said, ''I've never been out of Montana. Except now.''

Pathetic.

''Excellent,'' said Johann, slapping Conn on the back. ''Rome it is. I am sure Horatio will be excited to meet you. But, you understand, Edwina and Chad will not be there.''

''I understand.'' Though he was a bit curious about them, too. ''And my mom?''

''She will be under the best of care. She is one of us, Connor, and we will not see her suffer.''

There. That's all he really wanted to hear.

''Now,'' said Johann, leading Conn toward the study, ''let us talk about the future. We have so much to consider.''

Without translation, he knew exactly what was expected of him.

They were to plan how Connor was going to convince Lacey Vedae to give up the Spencers' land.

Their land.

The early afternoon sun struggled to melt the light
snow as Lacey arranged a new cluster of stones in
her rock garden.

The activity soothed her, took her mind off Connor
for a while.

Uh-huh. Sure. He was always in her thoughts, as
constant as the evergreens that filled her garden. She
only wished she could figure him out.

Why was it he still watched her with the same hungry gaze but, when it came time to go a step beyond
watching, he acted as if he wanted nothing to do with
her? Why had he been leaving her alone in her bed,
staying in his cabin as if they were polite strangers?

Something was wrong. Ever since Johann's cocktail party, ever since Mrs. Clyde had revealed her
knowledge. Every day brought new complications.

Lacey wished she could help with whatever was
taking him away from her.

There she went again. Worrying about everyone's
problems when she should be concentrating on the
positives. Her best friend was about to have a baby.
The glass castle was humming with visitors yesterday,
every one of them paying money to see the grand
sight in Kane's Crossing.

Word-of-mouth was working, spreading news of
the attraction. Her dreams for the Reno Center chil-

dren were finally coming true, in spite of Johann Spencer.

Life really was looking good.

A large shadow blocked the sun, falling over her hands as she finished setting the rocks into a balanced position. She glanced up, her heart giving a peppy leap.

Connor. His hair was loose, just how she liked it best. This way she could run her fingers through its softness, feel the strands as they floated over her face when he kissed her breasts.

"Hey," she said, a clear understatement.

"Hey." He didn't move, just watched her.

She, however, did move, standing in order to get a better look at him.

There was a hardness to his mouth, chiseling small lines into the corners of it.

"I haven't seen you around," she said, smiling in the face of his stern barriers. "Not since the day before yesterday."

"That's a stretch of time." His tone suggested a hint of humor, covered by layers of trouble.

"I'm used to seeing you skulking about, that's all." There. Be casual. Don't let him know how much your blood sings through your body when he's around. "So what brings you to my neck of the woods?"

Connor glanced away, then shrugged. "I saw you in this garden and… You know, it looks different during the day, now that I'm paying mind to it."

"Sunlight gives a different perspective on things."

He walked toward a stone lantern that was connected to an evergreen tree by a granite bridge. Ice was beginning to crack on the pond's surface, snow turning to rivulets running between the small stones gathered as if in contemplation at the water's edge.

"I suppose you don't see many rock gardens in Kentucky," he said.

Okay. So they'd talk about her landscaping. Merely having him near was enough, no matter the subject. They could talk about the contents of the phone book and it would be stimulating.

"Rock gardens are a form of art," she said, watching him roam the premises. "It's said there's no one way to arrange a garden, just as there's no one definition of creation or beauty."

He paused, then looked at her until she thought her knees would turn to slush. The intensity of his gaze was enough to make her cry with joy.

Or sadness.

She caught her breath. "They say rock gardens are a fusion of nature and architecture, a balance between nature and man-made magnificence."

"Lacey."

She stopped cold, knowing her Zen trivia was useless prattle, designed to put off the bad news his frown was sure to bring.

He walked toward her again. "I've been at the Spencer estate."

Should this make her happy? "Oh."

"I'm going to meet my father," he said.

"Congratulations."

Silence, filled only by a steady drip of melting snow, dropping from a nearby stone pagoda to a glimpse of grass.

"There's one thing Johann wants me to do for the family," he said.

Bad news comin', bad news comin'...

"And what's that?" She tried to seem unconcerned by bending down again, brushing snow off rocks with her bared hand.

"It's hard to say it."

"Listen, Conn." She didn't look up. "You've been distant since your first big meeting with Johann, and I know something's wrong. Spit it out."

A hesitation, then, "It's about the glass castle. The land."

Laughter shook her chest, uncontrollable, disbelieving laughter. She stood again, tired of trying to seem preoccupied. "What a relief. You, of course, told him to find the nearest cliff and jump off of it."

"Lacey..." He held out his hands, as if pleading with her.

"Right, Conn?"

He didn't say a darn word.

Lacey circled him, pushed by a head of steam, a thrust of anger so powerful she couldn't stand still.

"You know the castle is bringing in money? That, someday, it's going to pay for scholarships for the kids at the Reno Center? Kids who don't have parents to provide for them?''

"Yes, I know."

"That's what you told Johann. Right?" She went toe to toe with Conn. "Right?"

His shoulders lowered to a resigned slump. "He flew my mother here from Montana. He's hired a nurse to take care of her. He's making sure she'll have follow-up care from the best physicians in the area."

It was as if someone had sneaked up behind Lacey, grabbed her hair in a meaty fist, then twisted until the strands came out, one by one.

"Bluntly put, he's making you decide between me and your mother," she said. "They need you to persuade me to give up that castle land."

He shut his eyes, crossed his arms over his chest.

Wow. She couldn't feel hurt. The pain went beyond mere wounds, beyond stinging comebacks that would put him in his place.

"I hate this, Lace."

"Right. Did you hate seducing me, too? I mean, it must be mighty helpful to have already drawn me into submission with your bedroom charms. Oh, and the fact that I've confessed my love doesn't make wheedling the castle from me any harder. Does it?"

Connor's hand shot out, grabbing her by the upper arm. "Stop it."

She gasped, not because of the pressure of his fingers against her skin. But because of the heat of him, the current of his touch singeing her, burning her.

He lightened his grasp. "When you talk about that damned castle, you get this glow. I can see how happy it makes you to have accomplished something so meaningful. Believe me, I wish I didn't have to promise Johann that I'd talk to you about the land just so my mother can have some medical security."

Maybe he was right; she was being selfish. After all, what was a woman's life compared to a material object?

But the glass castle was so much more than that, and he knew it. It was every dream she'd had since getting out of HazyLawn. It was dreams she had for the futures of the Reno Center children.

"What if you can't talk me into anything?" she asked, her voice shaking.

He shook his head, not speaking.

Funny. Even though he was standing right in front of her, he was miles away. Untouchable.

Her fingertips itched to reach out, to run along the line of his jaw, the throb of the veins in his neck, the pulse of the skin over his heart.

"I'm losing you," she said softly.

He opened his mouth to respond, but Lacey already knew what he was going to say. She'd never had him in the first place.

Her cell phone vibrated against her hip. Ashlyn had told her she'd call if she went into labor.

As Lacey and Conn locked stares, she answered the phone, putting an abrupt end to their conversation.

Chapter Fourteen

That afternoon, Conn and Lacey had visited Ashlyn in the Spencer County Hospital, where she'd given birth to a son.

Charlie Reno, named after Sam's deceased father.

As the new parents had accepted congratulations from family and friends, Conn had forced himself to remain social, to offer support to his newfound sister. When Lacey had gotten the chance to hold his nephew, he'd almost choked on emotion, imagining a baby with his own eyes cradled in her arms.

A baby he'd never get to see.

Lacey had remained distant throughout the visit, standing on the other side of Ashlyn's bed, flanked by her brothers and their wives and children.

The message couldn't have been clearer. She was disappointed in the choice he'd made, and he couldn't blame her.

Consequently, Conn had visited Johann, related the news of Ashlyn's child and announced he wouldn't be putting pressure on Lacey to sell the land back to the Spencers. The sight of that imaginary future, the phantom baby, had been an eye opener, a real kick in the stomach.

Johann's jovial grin had turned cold. "We shall see how Seobain will manage her sickness, then."

It was an obvious threat. If Conn didn't do his job, his mother would pay.

As extra incentive, Johann had even added, "It would be a great tragedy if Ms. Vedae's castle was destroyed because of her stubbornness. Maybe presenting this option would aid you, Connor."

And it was with this "option" weighing heavily on his mind that Conn convinced his mother to stay at the Edgewater Motel then tucked her into bed. Afterward, he returned to Lacey's house, knocking on her back door.

When there was no answer, he automatically walked in, as he'd done many times before. Then, with a start, he recalled their afternoon meeting and how it had patently bruised her feelings.

Would she want him in her house?

A strange emotion stabbed him in the rib cage, in the center of his chest. He wanted to be near her. With her.

The hushed metal hum of water flowing through pipes led him down the hall, to a bathroom overlooking the rock garden. He knew from previous conversations and visits that Lacey loved this little nook of her domain.

The water squeaked off as he approached the door. It was partially closed, allowing a peek of muted candlelight to squeeze through the crack. A Chris Isaak CD played over some splashes, the singer's melancholy-smooth voice balanced by the soft twang of moody guitars and bass.

He stood outside. "Lacey?"

The rippling water stilled, as if she'd frozen at the sound of his words. "I'm taking a bath. Alone."

"Glad to hear it." He placed his fingertips against the door, as if touching the wood would somehow connect him to her body, her voice.

"No, I mean *alone,* alone. Without you." She paused, probably listening to see if she heard footsteps, if he'd taken the hint and left. Then, "You're not getting my meaning."

The numbness in his chest told him that he was. Getting it loud and clear. He just didn't want to leave.

"After what we saw today, with Ashlyn, with her and Sam and their new baby, I…" Why had he stopped talking? Where was his plain-spoken-ness?

She sighed. "Don't tell me. You had a life-altering moment today, and now you're back to being the man I first met." Pause. "Because I do miss that guy."

Pushing the door open a tad allowed more light into the hall. The hinges groaned a warning.

But it wasn't enough to see her.

"Let's get past everything that's giving us trouble," he said.

If she noticed his slow progress at opening the door, she didn't mention it. "I'd love nothing more, Conn. But I'm not sure we can erase that bane of my existence, aka Johann Spencer."

"I already have."

He stopped pushing open the door. From this vantage point, he could see the buttery hue of flickering flame against the shell-colored walls, potted plants lining the deep tub, a portion of the wall-sized window with evergreens providing shelter and a narrow view of the rock garden. He could also see the tips of Lacey's pink-painted toes, poking out of the bath's bubbles, resting against the porcelain edge.

He said, "You're never going to know the hell I've been through, trying to choose between you and my mother."

During the ensuing hesitation, Lacey's toes sunk beneath the waterline.

"I can only guess," she said.

She forcefully splashed some water onto the door. The drops tapped against the wood like a summons.

"Are you just going to stand there?" she asked. "It's not as if I'm a blushing virgin."

He tentatively opened the door, stepping inside the bathroom. The space was huge enough to hold a mirrored vanity table on one side of the room, closets on another, a bronze-fixtured sink with other accessories on the next.

But that's not what held his attention. Lacey sat in the middle of the tub, surrounded by mounds of bubbles—tangerine scented, if he guessed right. Her dark hair was tucked behind her ears, spiked with wetness at the ends. She hugged her knees, in effect covering her chest, while a dollop of bubbles sparkled on one cheek.

Desire roared through him, burning rubber through his chest, then lower.

Lacey's gaze took a leisurely spin over his body, coming to a stop at his own undoubtedly heated expression.

"I miss you," she said, leaning her cheek against her knees, those big gray-blue eyes resting on him, dragging him closer.

"God, me, too." He bent to a knee and dipped a hand into the warm, silky water. "Let's not talk about the Spencers tonight, all right? Let's just—"

She watched his submerged hand drift closer to her body. "—enjoy each other's company?"

He brushed against her upper thigh, and Lacey straightened at the contact, revealing the curve of her breast. He glided his knuckles higher, over her hipbone, her belly, barely skimming the thatch of hair between her legs.

Her sudden intake of breath was the only clue that

she was warming up to him, because the rest of her body was sure on alert.

"How do I know you're not going to try to talk me out of that land while doing crazy things to my body?" she asked.

"I thought you trusted me." He slipped a finger into the slickness of her folds, coasting back and forth. Her neck arched as she let go of her knees and grabbed the sides of the tub, her legs opening slightly, enough to let him know she wanted him to touch her, to love her.

"I need to trust you," she said. "Almost more than anything."

"Then let go, just for tonight."

"So you can betray me tomorrow?" Her voice came out on a gasp as he slid his finger inside of her.

"I don't want to do that."

In, out, in, out. The rhythm of his fingers and her body was causing the water to shift in the tub, rocking back and forth like storm waves. Some splashed on the tile floor, making a sound like a heart being torn in two.

"Remember," she said, stretching upward to wrap an arm around his neck, "I'm a businesswoman. You won't get anything past me."

She crushed her mouth to his as he supported her with his other arm, the material of his shirt soaked through, the stroke of his fingers increasing with the tempo of their tongues.

Water lapped at porcelain while her fingers raked

into his hair. He removed his fingers from inside her, traveling them up her skin, palming a slippery breast, feeling the budded crest of it nubbing into the center of his hand.

He wished the world consisted of Lacey. Only Lacey. Her exotic citrus scent, her serene gardens, her winning smile. Why couldn't he just steep himself in the warmth of her, drown himself within her moist heat, float with her in an empty silence while they touched each other's faces, never saying a word?

She felt it, too. He knew that. She said that she'd already fallen in love with him.

But he knew this moment couldn't wrap around them forever—this bubble in time in which she was pulling him down with her, into the tub, his clothes becoming saturated and burdensome.

He resisted, tugging her upward, out of the water, water sheeting from her body in a fall of drops. Her skin was slick, soap and bubbles making her slide out of his grasp as she crawled out of the tub, landing on top of him on the thick rug near the vanity table.

Their lips joined again, the kiss insistent, warm and breathless. He was so hard, getting harder, nearing explosion and total loss of control.

She leaned over, pinning his hands to the rug, stretching over him until he could take a breast in his mouth, licking it, tasting the slightly bitter tangerine bubbles in his mouth. She rubbed against the bulge in his pants, making him strain with need.

"I've told you I love you," she said, "but that doesn't mean I'm a pushover, Conn."

A thought flashed across his mind: love didn't exist. Not for him. Not since he'd found out his real father was a wife-cheating, baby-leaving jerk.

But maybe he'd found love here. Now.

With Lacey.

She combed her fingertips down his arms, allowing them to linger over his chest, his stomach. Then she shifted her hips, testing the stiffness of him, reaching down to undo his pants.

"I love you, Conn," she said, drawing him into her, leaning forward, back, rocking with the motion of the swaying bathtub waves they'd created earlier.

She was so warm, surrounding him, drowning him. Just as he'd wanted.

They moved together, Conn anchoring his hands on her hips, dragging her in an ever-quickening tempo until she reached her climax, falling forward over him, breathless and tender.

She helped him arrive at his own peak, and when he did, the room crashed down on him, pounding him into foam, smoothing over him and drawing him back into a big lonely expanse of blue nothingness.

As they held each other, she didn't have to say "I love you" again. It was evident from the way she snuggled her nose into the crook of his neck and shoulder, from the way she wrapped an arm over his chest, holding him to her in case he was torn away.

He thought that, maybe, he could believe in love. If tomorrow never came.

It was Saturday, and Lacey's volunteers had told her they expected a large crowd at the castle today. In fact, the numbers were increasing every weekend.

She'd be there, just to watch the children's smiles, the adults' return to a rainbow-misted place in their pasts. The faces, coupled with last night in Conn's arms, could fly her to the moon with the fuel of happiness.

Anything was possible.

As she sat on one of the benches the volunteers had installed so people could gaze at the castle in comfort, Lacey watched a gaggle of tourists marvel at it.

Boy, it felt good to know she'd done something so right. It felt good to know she still had some sort of connection with Conn, too. Maybe more now than ever.

Her heart thumped a little faster, thinking of his clothes puckered to his body from the bath water. Last night had been something, all right, though he hadn't said the one thing she'd been craving to hear.

I love you, Lacey.

Just four simple words. She'd said three of them enough times to beat him over the head with her feelings, but he still hadn't come through.

Was he holding back, just as she'd feared?

He'd left her bed this morning to visit his mom at the Edgewater Motel. Lacey couldn't begrudge him the need to be with the woman who was, unfortunately, in the middle of his emotional tug-of-war. Really, she was touched by his loyalty to Seonaid Langley, and she'd even offered to have her stay in one of her own house's rooms. But Conn would have none of it.

Deep inside, his refusal made Lacey wonder if he was already distancing himself again.

The lights seemed to dim in the mammoth warehouse, casting a shadow over the castle. Lacey wasn't sure if it was her imagination. After all, there was little natural lighting and the volunteers knew better than to fool with the switches.

She turned around, finding a reason for the darkness.

A mass of Spencers and their cronies had entered the building, their hands stuffed into the bulging pockets of dark coats, their bodies blocking the weak brightness from the entrance.

Johann speared the front of the formation, supported by his employees and…

Yes, of course. Conn was there, his arm linked with an older woman, one who seemed cheery and healthy.

Seonaid?

Instinctively, Lacey dragged her eyes from Conn in order to track Johann and his buddies. But then Conn spotted her and, with an almost imperceptible nod from Johann, ambled toward her, Seonaid in accompaniment.

The older woman smiled as Conn greeted Lacey. "This is my mother," he said.

They exchanged pleasantries, Lacey thinking, all the while, how happy she was for Conn that his mother seemed healthy. But what did she know about non-Hodgkin's lymphoma? Only what she'd read on the sly from the Internet and books, without Conn's knowledge.

And it didn't amount to a hill of beans when you compared her scant information to life itself.

Seonaid extracted herself from Conn's arm. "I'm going to enjoy the castle. Lacey, I admire the work you've done."

"Thank you."

"Now," she continued, "I'll leave the two of you alone." Much to Conn's apparent chagrin, she squeezed his arm before wandering off.

"Did she wonder where you were last night?" asked Lacey, testing the waters.

"She realizes that I stay in the cabin—usually." A soft smile formed over his lips, as if he was remembering that he *didn't* stay in the cabin last night. "You know, she's not kidding about admiring you. She respects your ambitions."

Lacey tried not to chafe at the way he'd danced around her reference to last night. "It's a plus to get that parental approval." Now, if only she could be sure about Conn's feelings.

He clenched and unclenched his hand. He obviously wasn't here for small talk or to relive good times with her.

Today was about business, no doubt.

"Well," she said, "we're back to staring at each other from opposite sides of the fence, aren't we?"

"No." He remained standing, looking as agitated as Conn could manage. "Listen, I've got to tell you something that I didn't have the heart to mention yesterday. Johann's disappointed I haven't talked you into giving up."

"Here we go again—"

"—Not that it matters to me." Conn took a deep breath, exhaled. "He's going to take matters into his own hands."

"Let him."

"I mean it. He hinted that something would happen to your castle if you don't give in to him." Conn spread out his palms, coaxing her. "Isn't it possible to somehow move it? Or...?"

"You've got to be kidding." Lacey stood, then brushed past him on her way to confront Johann. He'd gone too far this time, threatening her, casting negativity over the hopes of the Reno Center kids.

"Lacey." Conn inserted his big body in front of her.

For a moment, last night came between them, drawing them together. She thought she could even hear the echo of her heartbeat pounding his skin, but that was ridiculous.

He lowered his voice. "I'm not joking around."

"Have you become a turncoat?" she asked. "What would Johann do if he knew you were feeding me his plans? What will *you* do when he stops caring for Seonaid, or when he pulls the trip to see your father right out from under your feet?"

He stayed silent, the muscles of his jaw working.

Lacey shook her head. "Are you one of them now?"

It was as if identity had ghosted itself right out of his body. His skin paled, his eyes lost their luster. "I don't know who I am anymore."

She just stared at him. There was nothing else to do. After all the feelings she'd spent on him, after all the chances she'd given him to love her back.

"You have no idea how to return my love, do you?" she asked.

He glanced up at her, the shards embedded in the blue of his gaze exploding, just as a crash of glass shattered through the room.

She gasped, hand over heart, as if she, herself, had exploded into splinters, broken by the sound.

Johann, bordered by the other members of the Spencer clan, stood in front of the castle, his hand still poised from the rock he'd thrown at it. A turret bled crystals, and for one moment, one jagged piece balanced on the edge, then fell with the slow grace of a withered angel. It crunched to the floor, next to the other Spencers, who each held their own stone.

Seonaid stepped forward, voice raised, spreading out her empty hands. "What are you doing, Johann?"

The entire room had come to a standstill. One of the volunteers had even shut off the music. The rest of them stood frozen, never having been trained in this sort of scenario.

Lacey had never imagined someone would throw stones at her castle. Just at her.

Conn had already bolted toward Johann. Somewhere in the room, a child started to cry.

Johann held a hand against Conn, nodding toward the public. "This does not concern anyone but Lacey Vedae. Leave."

People began streaming out. As a volunteer passed her, obvious shame reddening his cheeks, Lacey said, "Call Sheriff Reno."

The man nodded, double-timing his steps. On the other side of the room, Conn moved to grab the wrist of a Spencer employee, one who had a stone ready.

"Let it go," he said, his tone cut with a threat.

The man did no such thing. He merely smiled and watched Johann for instructions.

The older Spencer sauntered forward, his eyes on the ragged turret. "Shame, really. It is a work of art. But there will not be much of it left if you remain stubborn in your desire to remain on this land."

Rage pushed Lacey's voice from her throat. "This is illegal, Johann. You'll never get away with it."

The man flicked a finger toward an employee. With obvious relish, he threw the next stone. This one decimated part of a wall.

Lacey felt the impact, flinching with the scream of

glass. She clutched at her sweater, right over her vaulting stomach. But she hadn't fallen apart—not yet. She was still standing strong.

A cut of ice rode the sharpness of her words. "Johann! I'm a civilized person, but if one more stone hits my castle, I *will* make you regret it." Her eyes narrowed, chopping her image of a smirking Johann in half. "And you'd best believe me."

As her voice carried through the massive room, her hands started shaking with pure terror at what she might be capable of doing to Johann.

Her eyes locked with Conn's. What should he do? he seemed to ask. He could take them one by one, but that wouldn't save the castle. There were too many Spencers.

Johann shrugged at Lacey. "This is how I negotiate, Ms. Vedae. Aggressively. I, and your castle, need your vow to sell the land."

"I told you," she said, "don't go a throw further." A deliberate smile—so cool, so calm, so filled with outraged promise—captured her expression. "You took great joy in taunting me about my challenges, didn't you? Well, maybe you should've been more concerned about my anger, because it's been simmering for a long time now. It's just been waiting for a low life like you to come along."

"*Lacey.*"

Conn had said it, his tone as soothing as a hand resting on her shoulder, and just as effective at blocking off more threats, too. Shame and relief mingled, trembling through her. Had she gone too far?

Conn's voice grew louder. "Johann, I'll throttle you before you strong arm Lacey into something she doesn't want to do."

"Connor," said Johann, "you talk as if you care."

The man she loved glanced at her, smiling sadly at her in the midst of the chaos. Lacey's heart fisted.

"I do care," he said. "I love the woman you're hurting."

He'd said it. Damn his timing, but he'd said it.

Me, too, she thought, a lone tear—one that had been collecting for a long time—sliding down her cheek.

Johann nodded at another employee. Another stone blew open a hole in another wall.

Without thinking, a horrific fury blew Lacey in Johann's direction. She aimed her nails toward his face, her vision clouded by disbelief and shock.

But Conn beat her to him. His fist thudded into Johann's belly, sending the man a few feet to the left, the force of the punch doubling him over as the Spencer employees surged over Conn, their black coats resembling vulture wings as they covered their prey.

Lacey pulled at them with all her might, and Seonaid ran over to help her. At the sight of the women, the employees backed off Connor, allowing Lacey and Seonaid to drag him away, blood trickling from his mouth, his eye already swelling.

As Lacey smoothed a hand over his brow, she

barely registered the background noise, the agonizing screech of stones hitting glass.

The sounds of her dream dying.

Conn's blood dripped from cuts on his lip, near his eyes, on his jaw. The wounds consumed all her attention, all her emotion. She dried the thick moisture with her thumb, soothing him the best she could.

"The Reno kids…" he said, trying to get up again.

Seonaid bent down to sit next to Conn, smoothing back his hair. "Johann's going to pay for this."

Yes, he would.

As Conn sat up, dabbing at his lip, Lacey stood.

She took in the destroyed castle, the piles of glass, the glimmer of lost money, the shards of all her best intentions.

Funny. The worst had happened, but it hadn't decimated *her,* hadn't cast her back into that dark pit.

She'd survived, and not a piece of her was missing or shattered.

"Congratulations, Johann," she said, her tone cold, emotionless. "You're a real man. A real Spencer. No wonder Ashlyn wants nothing to do with you."

Johann chuffed. "But Connor does."

Conn's voice rose above the destruction. "Go to hell—you and Horatio."

"Are you sure about that?" Johann cocked his head. "You seemed all too willing to join the family this morning, when you agreed to talk to Lacey about her foolishness again."

Conn got to his feet, and Lacey's heart caught in

her throat. Even bruised and battered he had the power to steal her breath away.

"You're not my family." He gestured to Seonaid. To Lacey. "These are the people I love. You and your money can take the low road to a place where greed matters."

Johann kicked at some glass. "Your words are empty. I am disappointed you did not live up to my expectations."

Conn stood next to Lacey, consoling her with his presence. He slipped an arm around her, strong as steel. Unbreakable.

"I'm only too happy to disappoint you."

In the distance, sirens screamed through the air. But Johann didn't run, didn't hide.

And when Sheriff Reno arrested him and his accomplices, they never even apologized.

Later, Conn watched Lacey hold a shard in her palm, looking at the glass as if peering into her broken hopes.

He kneeled next to her, picking up two pieces of his own. "I'm sorry."

His voice reverberated through the empty room. The volunteers and townspeople who had heard about the attack and joined the cleanup effort had left in tears after attempting to repair the damage. But Lacey had thanked them for their time and sweat, then told them it wasn't going to work, that it was an impossible effort. Amidst hugs and well wishes, she'd turned back to the jagged foundation of the castle, stone-faced.

At least the town had shown support, thought Conn as he'd lingered in back of the woman he loved, nursing his wounds, giving her time to grieve.

Now, she smiled at Conn, even though the corners of her mouth pulled downward. "You're not the one who threw the stones. No need to apologize."

He tried to piece the grooves of glass together, but failed. He tried again. And again. As if it mattered anymore.

Right. Like he could fix everything.

"Look," he said, showing her a close fit. "I'm getting there."

Lacey dropped her glass, then stared at the floor. "It's like trying to rebuild a fantasy."

"No, it's not." He rubbed the glass together, forcing them to match edges. "There. A perfect couple. Kind of like you and me."

"Yeah." A soft laugh. "We're a real pair."

"Hey, I gave up a wicked family for you." He tossed the shards away. "What a sacrifice."

"You can still meet your father, Conn."

He ran a hand over her cheek. "No, thanks. I meant what I said, even if I was slow to say it. I love you, Lacey."

Her face took on a luminous glow. Odd, how his love could make her so happy, could contain all the power to heal, to scrape the damage off the floor and start again. The trail of his words left a bubbling warmth in their wake, like sparks showering down after a burst of fireworks.

"I was so afraid," she said, her smile wobbly. "I thought, beyond friendship, that you'd never really love someone who had such awful burdens to overcome."

He rubbed a thumb over her cheekbone, just as he'd done the first night they'd met. But, now, there was no hesitation, no pulling back. "Your battle with depression?"

She nodded, glancing away. "I think the world of you. I did from the second you exploded into the cabin. I kept asking myself why a guy like you..."

"...would love a woman like you?"

"That's right."

As he cupped her chin, all the tension of the day ebbed downward in a wave of burning need, from his shoulders to the tips of his boots.

Conn grinned. "I was wondering the same thing about you. How did I get lucky enough to deserve this?"

Now that he was professing his love, the room took on a Technicolor sheen—the sun a slow melt of contentment, the blue-gray of her eyes a lavender dab from the palette of a painter's brush.

He wanted to watch the sun rise in her gaze every morning. Wanted to watch the moonlight slant over her at night as she slept. Wanted to cover her from darkness and fill her with light as he held her close.

"Lace, I—"

The tinkle of glass crunching under shoes caught their attention as Seonaid approached them, making her way through the damage. "I'll be waiting for you kids outside. I can't look at this anymore."

Lacey and Conn watched her leave, not saying anything until his mother vanished into a flare of sunlight streaming through the exit. Then, he picked up the glass again.

Softly, he said, "I want to marry you. I want to make you forget about what happened today, want to see you dreaming in your rock garden, want to eat your food and repair your roofs. Hell." He grinned. "I just want to wake up to the sight of your face next to mine."

Lacey's lips pressed together, and she glanced away, sending Conn into a near panic. Then she looked back at him, her cheeks flushed.

"About time you realized it."

He cupped her face in his hands, sealing their vows with a kiss.

It'd been so clear, but he'd failed to see through his own bleary-glass view of the world.

He hadn't found his identity in the Spencer family, not in Horatio, Johann's wealth or the plan to bring his mom back into the fold.

No. Lacey had brought out the real Connor, accepting him as he was—a simple country boy from Raintree, Montana.

He'd found himself in the reflection of her love.

Epilogue

The August sun had melted into the horizon hours ago, dragging with it the sight of green grass and sparkling summer lakes.

But inside the old Spencer toy warehouse, the new glass castle gleamed in splendor, not needing the magic of sunlight.

Lacey stood before the second coming of the Reno Center Castle, her arms resting over her chest, her smile as unstoppable as the driving victory chant of *Carmina Burana* as it played over the sound system.

Just as it had played during the first castle opening.

Conn walked up behind her and slid his arms around her waist. "Hell of a reopening. The best part of it was seeing the expressions on those Reno Center kids when they ran in here this morning."

Lacey turned her face to nuzzle her lips against Conn's jaw line. "Who would've thought that Johann Spencer's money could buy something so worthwhile?"

Both of them laughed. Johann had gotten his just desserts. He and the penitent Spencer clan had opted to rebuild the castle—on *Lacey's* land—instead of having to suffer the shame of legalities. When the town of Kane's Crossing had found out what Johann had done to the castle, the family had been browbeaten into donating more than enough dollars and effort not only to rebuild the attraction, but to cover any costs of Seonaid's medical expenses.

Not that the woman needed it. She was as robust as a horse, she liked to say, having moved from Raintree to Kane's Crossing in order to be with her son and daughter-in-law to be. She was on the road to a full recovery.

"So," said Conn, kissing Lacey softly, "this is where you want to get married, huh? No churches or traditional venues for you?"

"I've imposed enough tradition on us, I think. It's not every groom who'd agree to my courting conditions."

He laughed. "You're right about moving a little slower. We did go too fast during the first round."

Lacey felt herself blushing, remembering their lovemaking and how, after Conn had proposed, she'd told him she wanted to be walked down "Sweet

Lane,'' as she'd termed it. To stop and smell all the blossoming roses life had to offer.

''Is it too much to ask?'' she said. ''Flowers, candlelight dinners, strolls down Main Street serenaded by barber shop quartets…''

''I couldn't find one of those.''

''Well, we don't live in *The Music Man,* after all.'' She kissed his nose. ''You've been very sentimental and sweet.''

''Minute by minute you're adding to my male ego,'' he said dryly.

''This should deflate it. Are we going to invite the Spencers to the ceremony? Just to rub it in a little? Besides, I want them to see my one-of-a-kind wedding dress.''

An original. No more switching fashions, switching identities. She'd found herself in Connor.

For a second, his face went blank, and Lacey wondered if he had truly gotten over the fact that he would never meet his real father. Then he smiled, and her fears dissipated.

''It's tempting, but let's keep distancing ourselves from that branch of the family. Ashlyn's the only Spencer I want at my wedding.''

''You know how to make my heart sing, don't you?''

''That's because I love you, Lacey Vedae.''

He encompassed her in a kiss, swept her away into a place where nothing but the brush of his hair against her cheeks mattered. Even the darkness she'd been running from for most of her life couldn't touch her here. Not with his arms to protect her from it.

As the kiss ended, Lacey kept her lips next to his. ''I love you, too, Connor.''

As they held each other, a ray of light swayed over them, on its way to bathing the castle in brightness. Out of the corner of her eye, Lacey caught a sparkle, almost as if the glass castle had come to life.

Winking at her.

She winked right back, feeling as light as the flame of a candle as she embraced the man she loved.

* * * * *

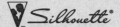

SPECIAL EDITION™

Available in February 2004 from bestselling author

Allison Leigh

A brand-new book in her popular
TURNABOUT series

SECRETLY MARRIED

(Silhouette Special Edition #1591)

Delaney Townsend was an expert at dealing with
everyone's problems but her own. How else could
she explain that the whirlwind marriage she thought
had ended definitely hadn't? Seems her supposed
ex-husband, Samson Vega, had refused to sign the
official papers. And the more time Delaney spent
with Sam, the more she wondered if the only
mistake about their marriage was ending it....

Available at your favorite retail outlet.

**Coming in February 2004
to Silhouette Books**

Abandoned at birth, blind genius Connor Quinn
had lived a hard, isolated life until beautiful
Alyssa Fielding stormed into his life and forced
him to open his heart to love, and the newfound
family that desperately needed his help....

**Five extraordinary siblings.
One dangerous past.
Unlimited potential.**

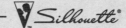

SPECIAL EDITION™

presents

DOWN FROM THE MOUNTAIN
by Barbara Gale
(Silhouette Special Edition #1595)

Carrying scars from his youth, forest ranger
David Hartwell had fled his home and settled in
the sanctuary of the Adirondack mountains.
But now, called back to deal with his father's will,
he was faced with temporary guardianship of
Ellen Candler—beautiful, innocent and exactly
the kind of woman David had always avoided.

Only, this time he
couldn't run away.

Because Ellen was blind.

And she needed him.

Follow the journey of
these two extraordinary
people as they leave their
sheltered existences behind
to embrace life and love!

Available February 2004 at your favorite retail outlet.